HYLAND'S PROPERTY

A RAGE AND REVENGE NOVEL

A DARK MAFIA DARK NECESSITIES ROMANCE
BOOK ONE

FELICITY BRANDON

PROLOGUE: SEAN HYLAND

Zander Hyland was dead. Not just dead but murdered—shot to pieces by the bastards that ran The Syndicate, or more specifically, one bastard, in particular, Saul Morrison. My hands balled into fists at the thought of the smug wanker strutting around London as if he owned the fucking city while my uncle was cold in the mortuary. I hated him. I loathed him for shooting Zander, for obliterating the only role model I'd truly had, but just as keenly, I despised him for bringing me back to the odious city.

I'd left London years ago, heading for the Riviera and applying every trick my uncle had taught me. It hadn't taken long before I'd had Nice at my feet, hordes of gorgeous, scantily-clad French women throwing themselves at me, men I trusted at my disposal, and enough money to afford those fast cars I'd always had my eye on. I took what Zander had started and developed the Continental division until everyone knew the fucking Hyland name.

They knew it, and they trembled at hearing it.

Nice had been my home, the only place I'd really loved,

and now, thanks to Morrison, I was back in the gray shithole I'd fought so hard to leave behind. Staring out the window of my private jet, I watched the monotonous rain lashing at the glass. London. It was just as I recalled it—just as grim and tedious, just as hopeless. In Zander's absence, the gang he'd kept so tightly leashed had unraveled, and they needed me. Many of them had been wiped out in the same attack that had taken out Zander. The details were sketchy, but I knew it was Morrison who'd pulled the trigger.

I knew I was going to make that fucker pay.

"Ready to disembark, Mr. Hyland?"

I turned at the grating voice of the air stewardess. She was pretty enough—they always were—but beneath the thick layer of make-up, she looked just as worn and tired as the rest of this depressing city.

"Sure." I rose from my seat, grabbing my briefcase and ignoring the way she batted her eyelashes. I had no time for a woman right now. There were men to regroup, vengeance to enact, and an empire to rebuild. "Is my car waiting?"

"It's on the tarmac, Sir." She flashed a smile. "I already had your luggage transferred."

"Thanks." I flung the word at her, an afterthought as I stepped into the English rain. Grimacing, I made my way down the steps toward the waiting Mercedes. Fuck, I hated this country. I couldn't wait to bring things to order and get back to the French sunshine, champagne, and sex. I'd always preferred things to be sophisticated and cultured, and that's what the French coast offered me—the privileges my family name afforded in the most beautiful of backdrops.

"Welcome home, Sir."

"Thank you." I nodded to the driver as I slid into the back seat and slammed the door. "Take me straight to Zander's place."

"Yes, Sir. May I be the first to offer my condolences? Your uncle was a great man." His head lowered. "He's greatly missed."

"What's your name?" I stared at his reflection in the rear-view mirror. It definitely wasn't a face I recognized.

"It's Cole, Sir," he replied. "Maurice Cole. I worked with Mr. Hyland for years, right up until the last day."

"Thank you, Cole." I smiled at the emotion in his tone. Loyalty like that was difficult to find and almost impossible to buy. "I'm looking for a good driver now I'm back in the country. Do you fancy the job?"

Cole glanced over his shoulder. "I'd be honored, Sir, thank you."

"Good, that's settled," I decided. "Take me into the city, please. It's time to get the wheels turning. Oh, and stop at one of those coffee shops, will you? I'm desperate for more caffeine."

The heavily made-up stewardess had already offered me more coffee than I should have indulged in for the day, but I never could get enough of anything I wanted.

"Of course, Mr. Hyland." He smiled, starting the engine. "It's good to have you home."

I glanced out the darkened window as we pulled away, amused someone was glad I was here.

CHAPTER 1: HILARY MANTLE

Checking my hair one final time, my gaze shifted to the reflection of the huge king-sized bed in the mirror. My boss, Saul Morrison, was sitting in it, his brow rising as our gazes met.

"Are you sure you have to go so soon?" He threw me one of those devastating smiles that made the muscles between my legs all clench at the same time.

"Yeah, I'm late for work, and my boss will tan my hide if he finds out."

Saul laughed at my quip. "I reckon he might give you the day off if you come over here and ask him nicely." One dark eyebrow rose at his assertion. "Especially if you ask on your hands and knees."

I ran my tongue over my teeth, imagining dropping to my knees and enjoying the things he had in mind. It was a tempting prospect. Saul and I had been dating for a few weeks, and even though bedding my boss was a dangerous game to play, the sex was fantastic. He was older than the men I usually went for, but that just made him better—more experienced, more considerate, and seemingly, it hadn't affected his stamina one iota.

"I'd love to, Sir…" I paused, remembering the huge pile of work waiting for me on my desk.

"But?" Saul sighed, sensing where the conversation was going.

"But I haven't been in for three days, Saul, and the work isn't going to do itself." I rose from the stool of the vanity unit and wandered to where he was stretched out on the bed. My gaze raked over his firm body, stalling at the erection straining to be free of his shorts, and fleetingly, I wondered if I was making the right decision. "I can come back later and help you with that, though. If you'd like?"

"Oh, I'd like." Saul was on his feet in a heartbeat, towering over me. "But only if you're sure. I know you have a life outside of me and The Syndicate, Hilary. I respect that." He reached for the side of my face, caressing my cheek, and my eyes fluttered closed.

How many days had it been since I'd gone back to my apartment? I could barely remember. Saul had everything I needed right here, and anything I requested was delivered in hours.

"I'd like, too," I whispered. "I'll pop home and grab more clothes."

"You won't need them," he promised, his lips grazing mine. "I promise to keep you naked and satisfied."

"Saul," I moaned as his lips shifted to my lobe. "You're not making it easy to get to work. Someone has to manage your diary while you lounge around all day."

He chuckled into the side of my nape just as one large hand slapped my skirt-covered backside playfully. I'd never relished being spanked before I'd bedded Saul, but he had taken me over his lap numerous times in the last few weeks, and I'd bloody loved all of them. The flesh beneath my office skirt tingled with the swat, sending electricity to my throbbing clitoris.

"Don't push your luck," he growled. "Or maybe I'll have to lift that pretty skirt and spank you in my office."

My eyes flew open at the delicious thought, his face rising to meet my gaze.

"That sounds like fun, *Sir...*"

"You are fucking insatiable." He sniggered. "But I have to admit, it sounds good. I never understood all the BDSM shit Connor and Dalton raved about, but you, Hilary, you make things so much clearer. With you, I want those things. You're delicious."

"Same here."

It was early days to be proclaiming long-term intentions, particularly to the man who signed my paycheck, but I couldn't believe how aligned we seemed to be. Saul was smart, respectful, attractive, and in control.

How had I been so damn lucky?

"Maybe I'll come to the office with you." He glanced around the room, his gaze landing on the large clock behind him. It was almost half-past nine already. "We can both catch up before we play."

"That sounds good," I agreed. "But I should go first. I have a mountain of work to tackle."

"And we wouldn't want anyone seeing us arrive together, would we?" His tone was sardonic.

"It's not that," I insisted, but it was. Even though we'd been sleeping together for weeks, and it was likely half The Syndicate already knew, I couldn't face the inquiring glances and the questions. Today, I just wanted to put my head down and catch up, so I could enjoy the weekend with Saul.

"It's okay," he chuckled, running his fingers through my

hair before he planted a chaste kiss on my forehead. "Go now, and I'll follow. Want me to get you a car?"

"No, Sir," I sighed theatrically. "I'll take the tube, like everyone else.

"Are you sure? I'm happy to get a driver for you."

"I'm sure. I've been traveling by tube since I was sixteen, Saul."

"I know, but now that you're linked to me, things are different." His thumb stroked my skin tenderly. "A man like me has enemies. It might not be safe for you."

I rolled my eyes at his appraisal. "Didn't you shoot your biggest enemy, *Sir*?"

His eyes narrowed at my sarcastic tone. "Yes, but there are others, Hilary. Our organization has a lot of fingers in a lot of pies, and just keep up that attitude, and I'll make sure I convene all my men to witness me spank your pretty arse later."

A shot of energy ran up my spine at his threat, pooling as arousal between my thighs.

"I'm sorry," I murmured, reaching for his forearm. "I'm just saying, I'll be fine, and anyway, we're not together, are we?"

He drew away, and just for a second, there was a flicker of hurt in his eyes.

"I mean, I love the time we spend together. You're great, the sex is amazing, but I'm just saying, we're not getting married or anything."

Saul's expression relaxed. "No," he agreed with a smile. "No marriage proposals on the horizon just yet, but I do enjoy spending time with you. I want more of it." He edged closer, pressing his body against mine. "Much more."

"Me, too."

I rose to my tiptoes to capture his lips, and growling, he pulled me flush against him as our bodies fused.

CHAPTER 2: SEAN

Glancing at my watch, my attention returned to the crowded London streets. It was even busier than I remembered when I was a teenager. Crawling through the near-stationary traffic was doing nothing to alleviate my caffeine-habit. Irritated, I searched the nearby shop fronts for any sign of a coffee vendor, and up ahead, I noticed an independent coffee house, Maisy's.

"Stop here for a moment," I instructed. "There's a place I can grab a drink."

"I'm sure I can find somewhere nicer, Mr. Hyland," Cole started. "If you just give me five minutes, there's a lovely little place that does the best cappuccino, and—"

"Cole." My tone was curt as I interrupted him, and instantly, his demeanor changed, reverting from the friendly staff member who wanted to help to the professional driver who'd served my uncle. "Just stop the car."

"Of course, Sir." Signaling, he pulled off the main road and skillfully negotiated into a space between two parked cars. "I'll wait for you here."

"Thank you." I felt for my pocket, ensuring I had my

wallet before I reached for the door handle. "If you need to move on to avoid a ticket, just call me. I assume they gave you my number by now?"

"Yes, Sir, I have it."

I just caught his words as I stepped onto the wet street. The rain had finally stopped, but the sky was still gray, heavy with the ever-present threat of another torrent. Pushing through the throng, I made my way across the sidewalk to the shop that had caught my eye, its burgundy awning declaring it offered the best coffee in London. I smirked at the audacious assertion, hoping it lived up to such high expectations, as I dived under the cover, narrowly avoiding the stream of rainwater pouring from a nearby gutter.

Fuck. Only a city this unappealing could have channels of water running from shop fronts, ready to drench unsuspecting customers. God, I hated this place, my every step evidence I was right—the grim reality was just as bad as I'd anticipated, maybe even worse. Anger simmered in my veins, and I shook my head at the ugly situation I found myself in. Striding toward the entrance, I hardly noticed the blonde darting in my direction. It wasn't until her high-pitched voice caught my attention I truly looked. Coffee in one hand and cell phone balanced against her shoulder, she wasn't looking my way as she skipped toward me. In fact, she scarcely seemed to register the presence of anyone else at all, but my gaze drank her in, crawling over the long legs accentuated by stiletto heels and the peachy little behind hidden beneath the tight skirt.

"Exactly!" she shrilled excitedly, speaking into the phone as she teetered on the patent shoes toward me. "That's what I told him, but he still wanted me to stay home, and, oh!"

In the haze of her eager conversation, she hadn't noticed me—the strapping, six and a half feet guy looming over her.

The one who hadn't taken his eyes from her since her timbre had broken his train of thought. As if to reinforce the point, she managed to crash straight into me, tipping her drink in the process.

"Excuse me?" I folded my arms across my chest, watching as the coffee made a track down my expensive white shirt. The heat of the liquid burned my skin, tightening my jaw.

"Shit, I'm sorry." Wide blue eyes met mine. "I'll call you back, Sindy. I have to go." She ended the call, slipping her phone into the purse slung over her shoulder, almost hyperventilating as she took in the mess her morning brew had made of my attire. "I'm so sorry."

"Do you ever look where you're going?" I arched an eyebrow, enjoying the bloom of heat that blossomed in her cheeks.

"I said I was sorry." Her free hand rose to her waist, her weight shifting from one hip to the other as she glared up at me. "What more can I do?"

At that moment, a host of suggestions of what she could do ran through my mind.

You can get rid of the attitude for a start. You can get down on your knees and show me some fucking respect. You can get out of that outfit and make my first day in London a whole lot brighter...

"You can at least be remorseful," I suggested. "And you can certainly pay to get this dry-cleaned." I gestured toward my chest. "The shirt was not cheap."

"I'm sure," she sneered, and as her brow rose, I saw a flicker of the woman she really was. Beyond the fine-looking exterior, the pretty face, the big blue eyes, and the cute little nose was a glimmer of the spoiled little girl who needed to be brought into line. My cock roused at that thought, an image of her chained by my desk flitting into my mind.

"Okay, fine. Leave me your number, and I'll arrange to get it dry-cleaned."

"No." My tone was absolute.

"No? But I thought that's what you wanted?" Her voice was indignant. "Wasn't that what you just said?"

"What's your name?" I glowered, daring the willful blonde to defy me.

"Hilary," she huffed. "Not that it's any of your business."

"Well, Hilary, it is now." I smiled at her. "Here's what's going to happen. You're going to give me your number, and I'm going to arrange the dry cleaning and bill you. Got it?"

Her jaw dropped open, and fleetingly, I contemplated which of my vast selection of gags would look the prettiest shoved in the space.

"I don't know who you are, but you have no right to talk to me that way."

"Is that right?" I leaned closer, only an inch, but based on the way I towered over her diminutive form, it was enough to garner her attention. Around us, other customers came and went, but Hilary didn't seem aware of their presence. Her focus was on me—just the way I wanted it.

"Yes," she snapped, although there was less conviction in her tone. "That's right."

"Were you not the one who blindly ran into me, Hilary?"

Her eyes widened imperceptibly at the way I said her name. "Yes, but—"

"Were you not the one who just agreed to dry clean the shirt you ruined?"

"Y-Yes." She stammered, decidedly less self-assured. "But that doesn't mean you can order me around."

Actually, Hilary, that's precisely what it means. My smile widened as the unspoken response swirled around my head, but somehow, I managed to resist the urge to vocalize it.

"Apologies if I came over a little severe." I thrust my palm in her direction, watching her breathing increase as she contemplated my huge hand. "I'm just used to doing things my way."

She laughed, the sound nervous, but in the end, convention won out, and my heart sped up as she reached forward to clasp my outstretched palm. She was so small, so fragile, and as my fingers closed around hers, so soft. It would be so easy to take over a woman as gorgeous and provocative as Hilary. So easy, and so damn satisfying...

"It's no problem," she replied. "I'm used to men who operate that way. Do you have your phone to hand? I'll give you my number."

"Sure." I reached into my jacket pocket for the device, watching the way her gaze never left me. "Go ahead."

"It's 07891 642361. Just message me when you have the invoice, and I'll take care of it."

I typed her number into my phone, imagining hot little Hilary *taking care of it* for me. Instinctively, I grinned at the idea. Boy, could I have fun with a woman like her, and now I was stuck in London, I needed a new distraction. Yes, work would be consuming, but there was nothing wrong with a little fun as well.

"Thank you, Hilary." This time I employed my most seductive tone, relishing the way she smiled in response, revealing the cutest little dimple in her right cheek. "Again, please accept my apologies for my harsh approach. It's no excuse, but I was recently bereaved, and I just arrived home to take care of the funeral. It's been a hard time."

"Gee, I'm sorry to hear that." She batted her eyelashes. "It's no problem at all. It was my fault, after all. I should have been paying attention."

"Then let's agree to start afresh," I coaxed. "No more apologies."

"That sounds fair." Hilary nodded, taking a sip of what remained of her drink. "Can I ask your name, though, so I know who it is when you get in touch?"

"Of course," I answered. "A beautiful woman like you should be wary of messages from strange men."

"Right," she giggled. "You can never be too careful."

"It's Sean, and even though we didn't meet under the best circumstances, I'm glad you ran into me today, Hilary."

She flashed me a grin. "Me too, but I have to run. I'm really late for work."

"Please, don't let me stop you." I took a step back, signaling for her to move past me. "I don't want you to get into trouble on my account."

Tucking her long blonde hair behind her ear, she glanced in my direction with a smile before she sashayed out of the shop. I watched the alluring way her arse wriggled as she exited the doorway, thinking how wrong I had been with my prior statement. I did want to get Hilary into trouble, and if I got my way, there'd be a whole lot of it coming her way. There was plenty she didn't know about me yet, but on one point, I was certain.

Sean Hyland always got his way.

"How was your coffee, Sir?" I stared at Cole as I settled back against the leather interior of the Mercedes.

"My what?"

"Your coffee?" He sounded bemused. "That was what you wanted to stop for?"

Shit, the coffee! In the frenzy of Hilary, I'd completely

forgotten the craving that had driven me into the local shop in the first place.

"I changed my mind once I was in there," I explained. "But not before someone managed to pour half of theirs over me." Gesturing to my stained shirt, I reached for my phone again, searching for Hilary's number.

"Goodness. I'm sorry, Sir. I'm sure we can find someone to remove that for you."

"Don't worry about it," I said, dismissing his concern with a flick of my wrist. "Just get me to my uncle's place."

My mind was whirring with thoughts of the woman who'd just coated me in her morning beverage. Sure, I'd had women before—plenty of them. There were young, attractive, leggy ladies everywhere on the Riviera, but there was something about Hilary that stirred me. Something that had planted a seed in my head, and it wasn't just her smoking-hot body. Her initial defiance had spoken to me, calling to the darker proclivities I reveled in when the urge arose. I had wanted to bring her to heel, right there in the shop, manhandle her to the car before I stripped and bound her, then once I got her back to my place, I would teach her what it meant to be owned by Sean Hyland.

I blew out a breath at the scintillating notion. There was no doubt, I had to see her again, but more than that, I had to have her. I had no idea if she was with someone, married, or maybe even a mother, but I didn't care. Hilary had run into the wrong man, then made another mistake by proffering her personal details. Her name and number alone were enough for me to track her down.

God help her when I did.

CHAPTER 3: HILARY

I'd been here for hours, stuck at my desk, working through the huge pile of admin that had accrued while I'd been tucked up in Saul's bed. I smiled idly at the thought as I hit send on the latest email. I didn't regret the time I'd spent with him, even though I was paying for it now, but I was a little resentful he could saunter in and out of his office while I was left here, picking up the proverbial pieces. Saul had swept into the building earlier, just as he'd promised, but there had been no time to play. As well as my enormous workload, he'd immediately been hit by the avalanche of people wanting to see him. Almost all the top team had stopped by to visit, and it had only taken one call from the Reilly's to ensure he scuttled off to touch base with them as well, leaving me here all alone.

Wearily, I glanced at the large clock ticking happily over my head. It was gone half-past eight in the evening, and even though I'd been late this morning, I'd still been here far too long. If Saul was going to be caught up in meetings with Dalton and Connor until late, I may as well just go home. I could grab the stuff I needed and meet him later. I stretched my tired limbs as the concept cemented in my head. It made sense. He was busy, and I needed to make the trip sometime. It might as well be now.

Logging off my computer, I grabbed my purse and headed for the exit. The foyer was busy as I made my way from the elevator to the door as groups of revelers came to enjoy the host of bars, clubs, and restaurants situated in the tower. Part of me envied them. I fancied the fine dining experience I knew Saul could offer, or perhaps even a visit to Diablo, the exclusive BDSM club run by Dalton Reilly. Smiling at the prospect of visiting there with Saul, I mused about how much I'd loved the bondage and spanking we enjoyed so far. I relished the way he wanted to control me in the bedroom, but beyond that, he treated me with nothing but respect. That was all I was interested in, where BDSM was concerned. I could never cope with any type of total power exchange, though I respected those who chose to live that way.

Stepping into the pouring rain, I immediately regretted the decision to go home. The paving stones were flooded, the result of hours of water falling from the sky, and the city seemed busier than ever. I'd never be able to get a cab, my preference at this time of the day, so with a heavy heart, I ran toward the nearest tube station. It took almost half an hour to reach my stop—twenty-five minutes crammed into a metal can with countless strangers, pressed up against men who needed to shower, with the obligatory crying baby screaming somewhere in the carriage. Scurrying out of the station with relief, I ignored the rain obscuring my view as I wandered onto the path. It was quieter here, as it always was, but it was also only a couple of minutes to my apartment. Skipping through the puddles, my mind wandered to my plans for later tonight. I'd pack a bag with the things I needed, then call a taxi to take me back to Saul. Reaching for my phone, I considered messaging him. Perhaps he would come by and pick me up after his meetings. The thought made me smile.

"Wondering when I'll text you?"

I started at the male voice, almost dropping my device in shock, but that was nothing compared to the surprise that hit me when I looked up to acknowledge its owner. There, under the covered archway and propped up against the double doorway that led to my apartment block, was Sean— the guy I'd bumped into earlier at Maisy's coffee shop.

"Hi, I..." My voice trailed away as I struggled to think of what to say. "What are you doing here?"

"I was just passing." He smiled, though something about the expression seemed rather too smug.

As though my body was trying to warn me, a shiver raced down the length of my spine.

"Here?" I asked, glancing up at the reassuring presence of the building I lived in. The sight of it was comforting, assuring me everything was okay. No harm could possibly befall me when I was this close to home. "Is this where you live?"

My pulse raced at the possibility Sean could reside here. I risked a quick glance at him under my lashes, reminding myself just how handsome he was. Dark-haired and incredibly tall, he had an air of sophistication about him I'd rarely known before, and his butterscotch skin reminded me of Saul's second in command at The Syndicate, Manuel. While Manuel was originally from the Mediterranean, Sean shared a similar bronzed look.

"Come in from the rain," Sean offered, gesturing for me to join him, and on instinct, my feet moved forward in his direction.

"So, do you?"

"Do I what?" He beamed at me, his deep blue eyes sparkling.

"Live here?"

I was nervous, though that made no sense. Sean was no threat, only a guy I'd encountered earlier. So, what if he'd turned up at my door? That didn't mean anything, did it? No doubt, I spent too much time with the men at The Syndicate and was seeing danger where it didn't really exist. Except, I couldn't shake that nagging feeling, and as he pushed away from the wall toward me, I had to fight the urge to retreat.

"You do, don't you, Hilary?"

Now, how did he know that?

"No, I've come to see a friend," I lied. "She'll be expecting me actually, so if you'd excuse me, I'll just—"

"I don't think so, Hilary…"

The air thickened with his words, and the pounding rain from beyond the archway and the hammering of my heart were the only sounds.

"What do you want?" My voice was weaker than I'd hoped, my teeth starting to chatter as water dripped from my hair. I'd been stupid to take the tube home. Why hadn't I just waited for a taxi? Why hadn't I waited for Saul?

"Just your time and attention." He edged closer, still blocking my route into the building. "You intrigued me earlier."

"Stay back," I hissed the words into his face, finally grasping some of the mettle I'd strived for earlier. "Whoever you are, you do not want to mess with me. My boyfriend is powerful, and he'll kick your arse." My heart threatened to jump into my throat as I threw the warning at him, my mind barely noticing the way I'd elevated the man I'd been casually fucking for the last few weeks into a long-term partner. It didn't matter now, and even if my threat had been filled with bravado, it was still true. Saul cared about me, and he was powerful. He would crush anyone who tried to hurt me.

"Is that right?" His dark eyebrow arched with the question. "That's good to know, Hilary. I've been finding out all sorts of things about you today, and now you just confirmed some of them."

"Wh-What?" I recoiled, stumbling back toward the street, no longer caring how it made me look. "What do you mean? What have you found out?"

"Just about your life," he answered with a smirk that suggested he was enjoying my response. "Where you work… and a little bird told me you were involved with a certain Saul Morrison."

My throat dried at the sound of Saul's name. "How the hell do you know Saul?"

"So, it's true then? You're dating the leader of The Syndicate?"

He was right on me, towering over my five-foot-five frame. Fleetingly, I glanced around, praying that somebody was passing on the street or about to leave the apartment complex, but there was no one.

No one to see me.

No one to help me.

"Eyes on me, Hilary." His deep tone drew my attention back to him. "I want your attention. remember, and you still haven't answered my question."

"You don't know me," I murmured. "What I do is of no consequence to you." I willed myself to turn and run, to flee from the bastard, and never look back. The tube was only a couple of minutes away, and there was bound to be someone around who could help me.

"Ah, but that's where you're wrong. It is of consequence to me. Everything about you matters to me now."

"Why?" I practically screamed. "Who the hell are you?"

It was then I heard the noise behind me, the sound of a car door opening, and the chance that some passing stranger could be my hero.

"Please!"

I turned on my heel, ready to plead with whoever was getting out of that car in the rain, but to my horror, it was another man in a dark suit, his expression somber as his gaze landed on me, and all at once, I knew he was with Sean. He was no friend of mine.

"Who are you?" I spun back to Sean, demanding an answer. "Who are you, and what do you really want?"

"There's no need to worry, Hilary," he cajoled in a tone that made me want to shudder. "My name is Sean Hyland, and I'm going to take care of everything."

CHAPTER 4: SEAN

I t had been pitifully easy to track her down. With Hilary's name, number, and my uncle's network of resources and allies, I had most of her personal details by midday. I discovered where she lived and had managed to bribe the security guard on duty to miss his shift, leaving her defenseless in an already undisturbed part of the city. After I'd convened with Zander's remaining men and taken stock, I took a little more time to investigate the enigmatic Hilary Mantle, and to say I'd been fascinated by what I'd found would be an understatement. Our chance encounter had been more fortuitous than I'd first realized.

Not only was she one of the most desirable women I had laid eyes on—the firm, slender body hiding beneath office attire and her feisty little attitude—but it transpired she was linked to the organization that had brought down Zander. By all accounts, her connections were not only professional. The rumor mill had it she'd been sleeping with none other than Saul fucking Morrison, and now the woman had more or less confessed it herself.

"Hyland?" Her brow creased as my family name registered.

No doubt she'd heard of Zander—they all had.

"That's right, baby." Reaching for her, my fingers slipped into her lush hair. It was soaked by the rain, but even damp, it was still the most delicious honey color.

"Get off me!" she shrieked, and in a moment of lunacy, she lifted her foot and sent the heel slamming down onto my shoe.

"Fuck."

I gritted my teeth at the pain, my fingers tightening in her tresses as my gaze lifted from her vexed expression to Johnson behind her. It only took one glance, and the good doctor was on the move, stalking behind her to ensure her fate was sealed.

Not that it hadn't been already. Little Hilary had been fucked from the moment she'd spilled her drink all over me.

"Do. Not. Do. That. Again." I punctuated each snarled word as I held her in place, tears forming in her eyes as she tried to resist the prison of my hand.

"I'm sorry," she panted. "Just please, let me go. I won't tell anyone. I won't tell Saul, just please—" She startled at the needle Johnson pressed to her neck, straining to be free of its intrusion. I captured the hand she rose to deflect it, holding her head and exposing her pretty little vein to the drug that was going to make her mine. Johnson was a qualified medic and had assured me he had a dose that would knock her out fast without doing any lasting damage. My gaze darted from the panic in her eyes back to Johnson. His judgment had better be spot on. I didn't want to kill Hilary, just take her for myself.

"Get off me!" She was crying now, all too aware of the peril she faced.

"Shhh," I whispered, releasing her hand to cover her mouth. "Not long now, and you'll be mine, little one."

"Is it done?" The question was directed at Johnson, who nodded as he withdrew the needle and assessed it in the damp evening air.

"Yes," he replied, slipping the needle into his pocket. "She should be out in a few moments."

Hilary's eyes were large at the statement, her hands rising to pry my fingers from her lips, but even as she tried, she stumbled, and I could see the first signs of the medication taking effect—the fight slipping from her, the light fading in her eyes as her uncoordinated body lurched forward.

"I have you," I murmured as she collapsed into my arms. "It's okay, little one. I have you."

"What have you done to me?" she murmured as I lifted her into my arms. "What have you done?"

I smiled down at her just as a couple wandered past with inquiring gazes.

"Is she okay?" the woman asked.

"She just had a little too much to drink," I explained with a warm laugh, watching as they smiled sympathetically before walking on.

Within minutes, Johnson opened the door and bundled her into the backseat. I slipped in beside her, waiting while he leaped into the passenger seat, and Austin Michaels hit the gas. Ten minutes in total to capture the woman I'd spent the day obsessing about, and now, here she was, sprawled over my lap, sleeping as peacefully as anyone I'd ever known.

"Where to, boss?" Michaels turned back to glance at Hilary before his focus shifted back to the road.

"Like we said," I replied. "Take me back to Zander's place."

It was mine now, of course. As his only living relative, I was due to inherit whatever remained, but things still seemed too raw to talk about the building that way. These men had worked for my uncle, and it would be *his place* for a while to come.

It was his legacy hanging over the area like a haunting.

"What do you have in store for her?" Michaels probed as we joined the main road.

I laughed at his audacity. "I'm going to keep her," I told him. "I decided I need a woman in this country, and I have little patience to wait."

"And what if she doesn't want you?"

"She doesn't get a fucking choice," I replied with a dark laugh. "The way I see it, the bitch is lucky I want her at all. I've saved her from the grasp of the prick, Morrison, got one over on the bastard, and got myself a pretty little plaything, all at the same time."

"Not bad for your first day," Johnson agreed.

"How long will it take for her to wake up?" I inquired, my attention slipping to her face once again. She was beautiful— pale, flawless skin stretched over high cheekbones. No wonder Morrison wanted her. It riled me he'd tasted the fruit that should belong to me, but there was nothing I could do to change the past. All I could focus on was the future.

Hilary was my future, and while I had to stay in this godforsaken city, she could help take the edge off and satisfy the darker proclivities that would require attention, now I could no longer frequent the exclusive clubs that had satiated my desires for so long. The fact she was Morrison's squeeze just made it all the sweeter. I could strike at him while I took my fill. I could taunt him with the loss while I marveled at the satisfaction of the gain.

It would be wonderful.

"Depends," Johnson answered with a shrug. "There's not much of her, so it might take a few hours."

"What about side effects?"

It was typical of me to query the point now that she was already unconscious, but that was the man I'd become. I was a shoot now ask questions later guy, with a proven track record in getting what I wanted. Nothing was going to change that. At twenty-eight, I was as set in my ways as Zander had been. In many ways, I suspected I was even worse.

"She should be fine." Johnson glanced back at Hilary's sleeping form. "Dehydration may be an issue, perhaps nausea, but nothing a little tender loving care won't rectify."

My brow rose at his assertion. TLC? That wasn't exactly what I had in mind.

"Just keep her alive," I warned him. "That's what I pay you for."

He smiled. "No problem, boss. She'll be fit enough for whatever you have in mind."

A dark rumble of laughter echoed around the interior at his comment as both he and Michaels mused on the notion, but the reality was neither of them had any idea what Hilary's fate would be.

Nobody did.

Except me.

CHAPTER 5: HILARY

Darkness. That's all there was, the breathtaking, encompassing darkness that swallows you up and threatens to drown you. That's what greeted me as I roused. Comforting at first, it soon became insidious, speaking of what was to come if only I could wake up and realize my predicament. My head pounded, warning me I'd had one too many drinks the night before, but as I strained my thoughts, I couldn't remember having a drink. Actually, as muted recollections materialized back, I couldn't recall drinking at all. I hesitated, pulling in a breath. Now that I thought about it, I couldn't remember much. I certainly didn't recollect meeting Saul or getting back to his flat. My brow furrowed. What was the last thing I remembered? I'd gone home after work, then what?

Swallowing back the rising anxiety, I tried to lift my hand to my temples and rub my sore head, but for some reason, I couldn't. I tried again, and still unable to move my right hand, I concentrated on using my left instead.

Nothing.

My limbs were not responding.

I could feel them, sensed my fingers straightening at my hands and the way my biceps flexed at my command, but for some reason, I couldn't connect the dots. I couldn't make those fingers and the muscles work together and lift my hand to my face. I tried my feet instead, but to my horror, the same reality dawned. I could wiggle my toes and circle my ankles, yet somehow, my legs wouldn't move beyond that rudimentary motion. Something seemed to be preventing me from moving at all.

Genuine panic bubbled inside, and a well of sickness stirred in my stomach.

What was wrong with me? Why couldn't I recall anything about yesterday, and more importantly, why couldn't I move?

Opening my mouth, I wanted to call out for help, but in the end, all that escaped was a desperate croak, my throat dry as I commanded my eyes to open.

"She's coming around."

I froze at the sound of an unknown male voice, my body all but paralyzed, save for my heart, which raced out of control.

"About fucking time."

Another voice. Oh shit, wherever this was, whatever had happened to me, there were two men, and I didn't recognize either of them.

"Is she okay?"

The second voice was louder now, its deep tone floating over me as I finally persuaded my lids to accommodate my instruction and flicker open. My breath caught at the sight that awaited me, and on instinct, they fluttered closed again, assuming this was all some type of awful bad dream.

"No, Hilary."

My body straightened at the sound of my name. Crap.

God only knew where I was and why I was here, but whoever these guys were, they knew me. A reflexive shudder shot up the length of my spine.

"Open your eyes."

I forced them to comply, eyeing the man who wandered into my line of sight and the darkened room behind him. No wonder the blackness had enveloped me. That's all there seemed to be out there—dancing shadows and dank air.

The guy was no one I recognized, his brown eyes and thinning hairline reminiscent of a thousand men before him. Lifting his hand toward me, he flicked on a small flashlight—the sort doctors sometimes used—and waved it in my direction. Head aching, I squeezed my eyes shut again, turning my chin to avoid the beam of light.

"The good doctor asked you to keep them open."

I leaped at the proximity of the second voice. It sounded as though it was being whispered into my left ear, and as my attention whipped in that direction, I came face to face with another man, a far more striking man, smirking at me.

"Who are you?" Somehow, I compelled the words out, even though my throat felt like sandpaper. "Where am I?"

He stared down at me, deep blue eyes alive with emotion as he spoke.

"Be a good girl and look at the doctor."

Wordlessly, his hands approached. I watched their progress with horror, my eyes widening as his fingers skimmed my cheeks, guiding my head back toward the other guy. Somewhere in my brain, I screamed at myself to resist him, to knock his hands away, but there seemed little chance of that. I still had no power over my limbs, and my head felt heavy as lead. All thoughts were scattered by the damn flashlight again, which the first guy shifted one eye to the other.

This time, there was no hope of looking away, held in place as I was.

"Reflexes look normal," he murmured, though I could only assume it wasn't me he was addressing. "Let's check her pulse."

Flicking off the light, he slipped it into his shirt pocket before reaching for my wrist. The hands at my face relaxed, enabling my gaze to follow his journey to my hand, and for the first time, I realized why I couldn't move.

Bound.

The word echoed around my head.

I was bound.

Bound to what looked like a chair, my arms fastened against the structure with thick leather straps.

Cold fingers slid to my wrist as my brain attempted to process the new information.

I was bound to a chair!

Why the fuck was I bound to a chair?

"Pulse is good," the first man said, his focus flitting to the one beside me. "How do you feel?" That question was fired in my direction, both of their attention searing into me, as though they expected some sort of damage report.

"Who are you?" It was easier to speak now, but no less painful on my parched throat. "What do you want?"

"Do you feel sick?" The first one inquired, ignoring my completely reasonable queries as his fingers left my flesh. "Headache?"

"Answer him, Hilary."

I turned at the demand, locking eyes with the one who seemed to be in charge, and fleetingly, something about him was familiar, though I couldn't put my finger on what it was. I certainly didn't know him. He didn't work with Saul, but there was something about him that seemed to make sense, something I recognized. My brows knitted as I tried to figure it out.

"Need a little help recalling what happened?"

I nodded, staring at his eyes as though his gaze had enthralled me. They were the color of the deepest oceans, mysterious and mesmerizing, and right now, that was as much as my mind could process.

"Answer the doctor first." He gestured toward the other man. "Then I'll answer some of your questions."

Looking back to the first guy, I pressed my dry lips together.

"I'm thirsty, and my head hurts. Can I have a drink?"

"That's not how you ask, is it, Hilary?" the one with the captivating eyes asked as the two men exchanged a glance. His tone was mocking, as though he was patronizing a small child.

"I don't know what you mean?" I felt my brow furrow as I tried to understand. It was as if everything was happening in water, each deed playing out in slow motion, my thought processes struggling to calibrate the unfolding events.

"Ask nicely," he coaxed. "If you're a good girl, things will be easier for you."

My gaze darted back to him, uncertain if I'd heard him right. Had he just suggested things would be easier? If I wasn't mistaken, that sounded like a threat, as though waking up bound to a chair hadn't already been a glaring omen.

"You know how to ask nicely, don't you, Hilary?" His dark eyebrow arched with the query, those blue eyes flashing, daring me to counter him.

I'd have gladly done so, too, if I could only figure out who he was and what the hell was going on.

"Please, can I have a drink?" I wondered if they were the

correct words, and the way his face relaxed assured me they were.

"There we go," he praised, reaching for the side of my face again. "I knew you could be good."

My instincts screamed at me to recoil from his touch, but for some reason, I didn't. I was still trying to understand why I knew his face. Why his bronzed skin was so familiar when it was clear it wasn't anything to do with Saul.

Saul.

The face of the man I'd been playing with for the last few weeks flitted into my mind.

Saul wouldn't have done this.

Saul didn't treat me this way.

"She seems to be fine." My gaze lowered at the doctor's appraisal. "Heart rate is up a little, but that's probably shock."

Probably shock? Was he joking? Whatever was going on here was scaring me half to death, and if I could ever figure it out, I'd have a mouthful for them both.

"Shall I get her a glass of water?"

I glanced back in his direction, wondering why he was seeking approval on the subject.

"Yes. Bring it here, then leave us. Hilary and I have some things to discuss."

The knot of angst in my belly twisted at the way he made that sound. I'd worked with The Syndicate long enough to know one thing—nothing good ever came from discussions where one person was tied to a chair.

The doctor turned, walking away until he reached the only visible door. As he pulled it open, a shaft of light filled the dark space, revealing more of the interior. It looked as though the room was abandoned, empty as far as I could tell, apart from the chair I was fettered to. As he pulled it closed behind him, the shadows rose once more.

CHAPTER 6: SEAN

"Have you worked it out yet?" I couldn't resist asking, playing with her a little, now that we were finally alone. "Do you remember who I am?"

It seemed Johnson had done his job. Hilary was alive, she was awake, and apart from a little dehydration, she was fine. My gaze slid over her bound form, my arousal soaring. Boy, was she fine. I'd removed her suit skirt and jacket when we got her back here, leaving her gorgeous body in its tight white blouse and tan stockings and garter belt before I secured her to the chair. I'd removed the heels, too, but mainly for my own protection. Hilary had already proven she was inclined to use her footwear in self-defense, and based on some of the things I was going to do to her, I decided to play it safe.

"No." She shook her head, her brow furrowing as her gaze fell to her chest. "I recognize you, but I don't know why, and where's my skirt?" Her head shot back to me. "Why am I half-naked?"

"That's an entirely different question." I smirked as I

sauntered around to fill the space Johnson had vacated. "Let's start with the basics, shall we—who I am. Any ideas?"

Hilary glared at me. "This isn't funny." She forced the words through gritted teeth. "It isn't a game. This is my life."

"Indeed," I agreed. "And it's going to go a lot better if you relax, do as you're told, and drop the attitude." I liked it, though. There was no denying that. I liked the mettle in the woman, the tension in her jaw and the venom in her voice, but I couldn't allow it. Hilary would come to heel. She was just like any other prisoner, anyone I'd held captive—bound by my rules and by the reality I decided—except the things I had in store for her were far more special.

"I…" She hesitated, and I could see the conflict warring inside her—her desire to tell me to go and fuck myself fighting with her self-preservation instincts. "I don't know who you are."

"Rule number one." My tone was even, practiced, revealing nothing of the excitement burgeoning. "From now on, you call me Sir."

"What?" Her wide gaze flitted to mine. "Why would I do that?"

I chuckled at her performance. "Because you're the one tied to the chair, darling. You're the one who has to impress me." Silence bloomed around us as she tried to comprehend her predicament. "Do you understand? I know what they say about blondes, but it's not true, is it? You're a smart girl, Hilary. You get it."

"Yes." Her voice was quieter, her gaze falling to her stocking-clad knees as I waited for the word that would make my cock harden and my heart sing. To my absolute irritation, it didn't come.

"Yes, what?"

I leaned closer, my voice clipped. I wanted Hilary, but I

wasn't a monster. I would make it good for her, so long as she played the game. Showing me the appropriate level of respect was the first step on that journey.

"Sir." She never lifted her chin to meet my eyes, but it didn't matter—she said it. There would be time for finesse later.

"Good. So now to my question. Know who I am yet?"

Curious blue eyes were back on me in an instant, adorned by the delightful blush blooming on her cheeks.

"No, Sir."

"Want me to help?" I offered her a smile not only as reassurance, but frankly because I was enjoying myself, and it was only just the beginning. "We met yesterday in a little-known coffee shop called Maisy's."

Her eyes widened perceptibly, the wheels in her head, presumably starting to turn.

"Oh God," she croaked. "You were the one I ran into. You were going to message me about your dry cleaning."

I laughed gently at her recollection. "Yeah, well, let's just say I'm less concerned about the dry cleaning now."

I lowered to my haunches, my gaze raking over her bound body. Not only were her hands secured on the armrests, her ankles were bound to the bottom of each side of the chair as well, making escape all but impossible. Her thighs strained to close under my surveillance, but the position of the bondage meant that was hopeless as well. There would always be a few inches for me to play with, those inches currently offering me a tantalizing glimpse of her panties. I'd been a good boy, resisting the temptation to play with her while she'd been unconscious, but now she was awake, it was a different matter.

All bets were off for Hilary.

"What do you want from me?"

I waited a few seconds for her to give the address I'd asked for.

"Sorry, what was that?"

She sighed, her shoulders dropping in defeat. "Sir," she practically spat the word. "What do you want with me, Sir?"

"Your compliance, your obedience..." I paused as our gazes met. "You."

"Me?" She gasped, pushing her breasts toward me as her chest filled with air. "Are you going to kill me?"

"Kill you?" I couldn't help laughing at her conclusion. Clearly, she had worked for Morrison for too long. "Now, why would I want to do that?"

"You kidnapped me," she started. "You have me tied up in the dark. It..." She paused, her eyes gazing around the room I had chosen for her initial captivity. "It doesn't bode well."

"Rule two." I leaned even closer until there was only a matter of inches between our faces. "Listen to me, Hilary. I already told you how I needed you to behave, didn't I? I told you to be good and obey me, then I can make things better for you."

She blinked, her warm breath washing over me.

"Are you going to hurt me, Sir?"

My balls ached at her plea, but I pushed the soaring arousal down.

"Not if you do as I ask," I assured her. "I just wanted some company, but once I dug a little deeper into your online profile, I found out something else. Something that makes you infinitely more worthwhile to me alive."

"What?"

My brow arched at her missing word. If Hilary was going to be this remiss with my simple instructions, I would help her focus.

"Sir." She added it just in time to save herself.

"I found out you worked for Saul Morrison and allegedly have been fucking him."

Her pretty features screwed into a ball. "Yes, I work for him," she hissed. "The rest is none of your damn business. I don't even know who you are."

I reached for her, burying my fingers in her soft tresses.

"Then you weren't paying attention, little girl," I murmured. "I already told you, and you should watch your tone."

Panic pinballed in her gaze as my digits tightened. "I-I don't remember. I'm sorry."

"The after-effects of the sedative, perhaps," I mused aloud. "Okay, I will offer this one reprieve, Hilary, but think carefully before you speak to me that way again."

She nodded as best she could with my fingers buried in her hair.

"I am Sean, and Zander Hyland was my uncle. The only reason I'm back in this shitty city is Saul Morrison shot him."

A glimmer of recognition flickered in her eyes.

"What does that have to do with me, Sir?"

"Everything."

I eyed her lips, considering kissing her, but thought better of it. This wasn't the time for shows of ill self-discipline. Hilary was exhausted, dehydrated, and no doubt, confused as she attempted to piece together the jigsaw of recent events. There would be a time to claim her, to take the caress I wanted, but that time wasn't now. My initial impulses had been to take her for the one thing I badly wanted, but having her gave me a new perspective. Hilary wasn't going anywhere, so why not play the long game? I could take any woman and fuck her, but holding Hilary, I realized I could have much more than that.

I could get inside her head.

I could make her want me, too.

I could truly make her mine.

Wouldn't that be the best dose of revenge as far as Morrison was concerned? To make it evident to him, I could not only make his woman my captive, but I could captivate her as well.

It would be perfect.

"You are everything," I reiterated. "I thought I only wanted a lover, someone to amuse me while I'm stuck in London, but having you here has made me rethink. Maybe I need more than just a plaything. Maybe it's time things got serious."

The words were falling from me now like rainwater from an open gutter, and even I didn't know how sincere I was at that moment, but I liked the shocked expression on her flawless face, the way she struggled in the binds, and the desperate tone when she answered.

"Wh-What do you mean, serious?"

"What was that?" My tone was curt, though holding her head just where I wanted it, I grazed my mouth over her half-open lips. "I didn't hear you, baby."

"Sir." Her body recoiled to the back of the chair, but of course, there was nowhere for her head to go. She was trapped in the prison of my design. "What do you mean?"

"I mean, I intend to make this a permanent arrangement, Hilary. The longer-lasting, the better. Morrison doesn't deserve a woman like you, and a woman like you doesn't merit scum like him."

"Scum?" Her brow creased. "He's not scum."

"He killed my uncle." I drew away from her, scowling at her response. "Shot him at point-blank range."

"I don't know all the things that went on," she mumbled,

"but he always treated me well." She glanced around. "He never tied me up in some crappy room."

"More fool him." I rose to my full height, folding my arms across my chest. "Right now, you're proving that's precisely the treatment you need to rid you of this petulance."

"Petulance?" she hissed accusingly. "You kidnapped me! You stuck *me* with some goddamn needle!"

"Keep it up!" My brow rose at her tone, fury simmering in my veins. Hilary would need to learn her place, and she needed to learn it fast. I had no idea what kind of shit show Morrison ran on the other side of the city, but I wasn't going to stand for her insolence. "You'll earn yourself even more time in my chair."

"Fuck you!" She pulled against the leather at her wrists, grunting with frustration. "You can't keep me here. Saul will find me, he'll find me, and he'll come for you."

That was it. I had heard enough.

Reaching inside the pocket of my Versace jacket, I fingered the outline of the ball gag, the smallest one on the market, but it would still do its job perfectly. Hilary might look great, but her constant whining was giving me a headache.

"Is that right?" I took a step toward her, looming over her bound form. "You think lover boy will be able to track you down? You think he'll give a shit?"

She rolled her shoulders back, glaring up at me.

"Damn right, I do," she snarled. "Saul cares about me. I'm not just a piece of property he can drug and contain. He respects me."

I laughed at that. Respect? What did the long-legged blonde know about respect? Hell, she'd been full of it from the first moment I'd laid eyes on her. There was little doubt —Hilary had this coming.

"Well, good for him," I replied, circling her body. "Tell me, how does he respect you?"

Naturally, I didn't give a damn how he treated her, but querying his behavior would give her another excuse to wax lyrical and me the opportunity to get the ball gag where it needed to be—shoved between the teeth of pretty little Hilary.

"He asks for my opinion," she started. "He takes care of—"

She never had the opportunity to complete that sentence. Turning on my heel, I swiped the gag from my pocket, grabbing the length of leather in both hands and lifting it up and over her head. By the time Hilary saw it coming, it was too late—I had the gag in place, the ball sliding into her mouth as she screeched behind it. I smiled, tightening the buckle at the back of her hair before I wandered around to appraise her.

"Very nice," I cooed.

Bound and gagged, Hilary looked seriously sensational.

"Here's the water."

I spun at the sound of Johnson's voice to find the older man lurking in the corner with a glass. He took one look at Hilary, brow rising.

"What the hell happened, boss? How is she going to drink like that?"

"She's not." It wasn't ideal, of course. Hilary needed the water, but then, I had needs, too. I needed to send a clear message about the rules, about what was acceptable, and mouthing off about her former employer while disrespecting me had overstepped too many lines. She could drink later. When I decided it was time. "Give it to me."

He walked over, thrusting the glass into my waiting hand, and I lifted it to my mouth before taking a large gulp. Hilary yelled behind the plastic once more, most of her consonants lost as she expressed her dissatisfaction with my decision.

"What was that?" I probed sardonically. "It's impossible to understand you when you're gagged, baby, but that's okay. I know you want the rest of the water, and don't worry, I'm going to give it to you."

Stepping forward, I threw the remainder of the glass's contents at her chest, the water soaking through her tight, thin shirt. She shrieked at the drenching, her stunned gaze lowering to her chest at the same time mine did—just in time to notice the material become translucent, soaking through her bra and revealing her pebbling nipples. My cock swelled at the blissful sight.

"My my." I cooed. "It's like a wet tee shirt competition in here, except there is no competition, darling. You win."

She narrowed her eyes, all four limbs struggling against the leather.

"Johnson." I turned to see his grinning face. It seemed he, too, was relishing the show. "There should be some scissors in the cupboard over there. Would you mind grabbing them for me?"

"Sure, boss." He strode toward it just as Hilary began to pant, the unmistakable sounds of pleading coming from behind the plastic ball.

It was too late.

Far too late.

Little blondes who upset me paid the price, and as Hilary was about to find out, the cost could be high.

CHAPTER 7: HILARY

Watching the doctor pass the scissors to Sean, my insides tightened. The son of a bitch had me tied to a chair, and now, just to exacerbate my circumstances, he'd gagged me as well. There was nothing I could do to fight back—no way of resisting. I struggled against the plastic in my mouth, pulling hot ribbons of air through my nostrils. To think I'd actually been curious when Saul had suggested we play with a gag. I'd been horny at the idea, but now that there was one shoved unceremoniously between my teeth, things were different. There was nothing sexy about this. Nothing good about the way I couldn't vocalize my concerns, nothing alluring about the way my chest was freezing with cold water, the fabric sticking to my skin, and even less appealing about the way Sean towered over me, scissors in hand.

"What are you going to do, boss?" The doctor sounded almost excited, but Sean's expression remained solemn.

"I told you, anything I fucking like."

My heart hammered at his verdict, but I fought to control

my responses. Whatever he was going to do, I didn't want to give the satisfaction of knowing I was petrified.

"It's time to help Hilary out of those wet clothes." Sean smirked, opening the arms of the scissors as he moved toward me. "After all, she'll get cold in this state."

My gaze followed as the blades approached my left shoulder, tension peaking in my body until I felt as if I might burst, but other than thrash around in the chair—a deed which clearly entertained both of them—there was nothing I could do to halt the attack, no way of saving myself.

"Don't worry, baby." Sean's tone was a soft, annoying purr again, the one that meant I could happily throttle him. "This isn't going to hurt."

He pinched the edge of my blouse, where the bodice met the sleeve, and snipped into the material. A part of me was horrified at the criminal damage, but another, larger facet was simply relieved as he angled the blades down the hem and proceeded to remove the sleeve from the rest of the top. Of course, the sleeve still encased my arm, but it was no longer connected to the rest of the shirt. Panting, I watched as he ambled to my other arm and began the process again. In a couple of minutes, neither sleeve was attached to my blouse.

"Almost there." Sean smiled down at me, revealing a row of pearl-white teeth. "Just a few further adjustments to make."

Leaning over me, he grabbed the drenched fabric clinging to my left breast, easing it away from my skin from the hem he'd just created at my shoulder. He slid the scissors a few inches beneath the material before pushing one blade up through the fabric. My gaze darted to his face as he slashed the thing, angling the blades until he cut a semi-circle. It took a few seconds for me to understand what he was doing. My attention was fixated on the scissors cutting so close to my skin, but he never hurt me, working meticulously until a complete circle had been cut around my breast. Snipping away the final piece of fabric connecting the circle to my blouse, he grinned, lifting the wet material to my face.

"One." His eyebrow arched, and he threw the cloth to the floor with a laugh before he edged closer to my right shoulder.

This time, I knew precisely what he was going to do, but bound and gagged, there was nothing I could do to prevent the hooliganism. Forced to be passive, a submissive observer, I watched as he recklessly attacked the other side of my shirt until finally, there were two large circles cut from the front. I stared down at myself, close to hyperventilating as my gaze absorbed the sight. My lacy bra was visible on both sides, my buds still aching from the cold.

"And two." Sean smiled, stepping away as if contemplating a piece of artwork. "Beautiful, but I think it still needs improvement."

Waving the scissors in front of me, he approached again, a diabolical grin on his face.

"No!" I screeched around the gag, but all he did was shake his head, tapping the plastic ball before pressing his index finger against it.

"Hush," he warned. "You don't want me to find a bigger gag for you, baby."

His large fingers landed on my breast, caressing a gentle line over my sodden skin before one, then two, hooked beneath the lace.

"No!" I couldn't help calling out again, my gaze flitting north to meet his arrogant expression.

"Yes, darling."

Sean held my gaze for a moment longer before his focus

fell back to my bra, then wordlessly, he sliced the lace away to reveal my breast—damp, exposed, and utterly vulnerable.

"Beautiful." His tone was almost reverent as he grazed a thumb over my goosing skin. "Just as I knew you'd be."

"Fuck you!" I snarled, gag or no gag, and based on the way he flinched, I reckon he deciphered the words.

"Language, Hilary." He tutted, gaze narrowing before his fingers rose to my defenseless nipple and pinched.

I gasped at the sudden hurt, trying in vain to shrug him away, but it was futile. Sean had access to my body, whether I liked it or not, and to make matters worse, the smirking doctor was a witness to my ordeal. Sean had inferred he should leave, but the doctor was still there, grinning behind him. Indignation burned in my veins, the emotion almost as incessant as the burgeoning dread. The hand that violated me skimmed a line up my flesh until it cupped my throat. Long fingers grasped at my windpipe, the pressure mild but insistent.

"You don't want to get on my wicked side, little girl. That would be a bad idea, a very bad idea indeed."

He held me there for a moment, frozen in time as his gaze burned into mine. Exposed and humiliated, I had nothing to offer in return, the thrumming alarm and pounding of my heart the only reminders I was really alive, and this wasn't one awful nightmare.

Then, just as I was certain I couldn't take anymore, the hand slipped away, his attention returning to my other cup, and silently, he worked to cut it, ripping the final part of the lace from my body to leave me bare and vulnerable.

"Very nice." The doctor's voice floated through the air, but I couldn't lift my eyes to meet his gaze. Embarrassment burned at my cheeks at the ignominy, the fact I was first bound, then gagged, and now, helplessly exposed blooming as a hot blush.

"Better than that," Sean countered, handing the scissors back to him. "She's fucking amazing, and only one thing is going to make this picture better."

Reaching into his jacket pocket, a sudden wave of fury flowed through me.

How dare he do this!

How dare he take me and treat me this way. Saul was going to rip his fucking windpipe out and beat him to death with it when he found out. The thought was comforting, buoying me as his hand reappeared, this time with two wooden clothespins.

"Know what these are for, beautiful?"

I dragged my gaze to meet his smug expression. The arrogant prick might have me at his mercy, but my terror would be short-lived. I couldn't wait to see what Saul would do when he found out about my kidnapping.

"No?" Getting no response, he edged closer, one large hand closing around the clothespins. "Then let me show you."

Collecting one pin from the other hand, his fingers drew the wooden arms open and slowly pressed the thing toward my chest. With my nipple pebbled from the temperature and exposure, it was flagrantly obvious what he had in mind, but worse, I was powerless to prevent him from achieving it. There was no choice but to gasp as the wood closed around my nipple, the arms pinching it hard as Sean relaxed his grip.

"Perfect." He laughed, glancing over his shoulder at his odious friend. "At least it will be when the other one is in place."

I fought this time, struggling against the leather that held my wrists and ankles in place, even though I acknowledged it was futile. Even though I knew I could never overcome, somehow, it was too important not to try, but in the end, my attempts were met with failure. Sean attached the second clothespin to the other nipple, the initial burst of pain capturing my attention before I noticed what he was doing next.

One more reach into that blasted pocket revealed his cell phone. He waved the device in the air mischievously before stepping back to capture the look of me.

"Here she is, Morrison." He growled the words while he hit record, sneering at me from behind the screen. "This is the fate of your lover, except by the time you see this, she won't be your lover at all. She'll be mine."

CHAPTER 8: SEAN

She was wonderful, her features screwed into a ball as I concluded the recording, her body still fighting against the bondage, and every time she writhed, her breasts bounced delightfully in the underwiring of what remained of her underwear. Like every schoolboy's wet dream, Hilary was bound in the gloom and entirely at my mercy.

She was mine.

"Now, now," I purred. "Don't be too hasty to judge me. I may not be your average host, but who wants to be average?" I smirked at my own joke, though her expression only hardened, a string of fresh mumbles coming from behind the gag.

"You know I can't understand you properly, darling," I said with a shrug as I slipped the device away. I'd make sure it was sent to Morrison. Knowing he was aware of her fate would be the cherry on the already generously iced cake. "Let me put it this way. Yes, I have you. Yes, I expect you to obey me, but I am going to make it good for you."

I stepped closer again, dodging the clothespin and trailing one finger under the curve of her breast. I had always admired a pair of nicely clamped tits, and these wooden pegs were the perfect introduction. Soon, I'd introduce Hilary to my favorite crocodile clamps. My grin widened at the prospect of how fucking good they would look on her wonderful breasts. Full, yet pert, they were some of the best I'd ever seen, and God knew, I had seen a few.

"I had the chair made specially for you." Her enraged gaze rose to meet mine, her gaze widening ever so slightly at my admission. "Let me show you." Glancing over my shoulder, I gestured for Johnson. "Let's get some light in here. Hilary is going to put on a show for us."

I laughed when she thrashed harder, ignoring her response while Johnson complied. With only one slit of a window, this was the perfect interrogation room, but it made exhibiting my new prize difficult. I wanted to glory in what was mine.

I wanted to show her off.

She blinked hastily as spotlights illuminated from the four corners of the room. There were others above her head, but wisely, Johnson hadn't activated those yet.

"That's better." I smiled at her concerned expression. "Now, to get you comfy."

I strode around her body, surveying the mattress behind her. Everything was in place for what I had in mind next. Stepping onto it, I grasped the back of her chair and braced, slowly easing it backward, Hilary and all. She cried out as I tipped her, the panic understandable, although she was in no danger. I didn't blame her for not believing that concept, though. So far, the man she'd bumped into at the coffee shop had turned up at her apartment building, injected her with an unknown drug, and she'd woken up here in the squalor of the room where I usually hosted my unwitting enemies.

"Calm down." I eased her back onto the mattress, her

head resting against the thing, her legs forced into the air. "You're safe. Nothing bad is going to happen to you."

Though *bad* was a relative term.

"This chair has some special adaptions, Hilary. It's not just for binding pretty little things, it's for pleasuring them, too." My gaze drilled into her with the declaration, and I watched her responses carefully. "I want to show you that life with Sean Hyland won't all be bad—if you do as you're told, I can make it pretty damn incredible."

Her brows furrowed at that suggestion, a litany of objections burning in her eyes, none of which she could vocalize with the plastic shoved between her teeth.

I turned to the seat her perfect little arse was squashed against, or more precisely, to the alteration I'd had made to it. Reaching under the chair, I unlocked the middle section, easing it to the floor. With the center removed, Hilary was now effectively bound to two separate leg rests, her pretty little panties clearly visible as she squirmed below me. I smiled at the pleasing sight. It wasn't enough to have Hilary here like this. I wanted her wet and desperate, and the new design, coupled with the massive vibrator I had stored away for the purpose, would accomplish that. She might think she hated me—she probably did—but I was going to squeeze more orgasms from the woman than any man had done. I'd eclipse anything Saul fucking Morrison could achieve.

"Ready for my next trick?" I knew this was only a one-way dialogue but relished it, nonetheless.

She shook her head, apparently keen to assure me she wasn't ready, but the best was yet to come. Sauntering to the cupboards on the right wall, I opened the door of the first to reveal the sleek, black vibrator I'd bought for the occasion. If there was one good thing about London, it was the multitude of adult stores. There was a sex shop on every street corner, and one of Zander's minions had happily visited one to make the purchase. Reaching for the toy, I grabbed the pink bondage tape I'd also acquired and wandered back to my girl. Practically hyperventilating, she eyed the objects in my hands with morbid fascination, her arms fighting all the harder as she took in my choices.

"See," I told her triumphantly. "Nothing to worry about, baby. I'm just going to give you a little fun."

Kneeling beside her, I set to work. In another time, with another woman, I'd have removed the lacy panties that hid her sex from me, but Hilary was different. I'd decided she was one I intended to keep, and I didn't want the pussy I owned flashed around for any of Zander's men to enjoy. They would get a good display as it was. That's why I left the skimpy lace in place as I positioned the vibrator over her pubis. The new purchase had a curved design, cocooning her body perfectly—the head nestling between her tantalizing lips while the remainder rested on her flesh. Christ, I envied the thing. I wanted to be between her legs, exploring her fabulous cunt, but I would have to wait my turn. Fucking Hilary would be all the sweeter once she was begging me for it, once she begged for relief from the vibrator.

"Now, just a little tape to hold it in place," I explained, ripping an ample piece from the reel. "I don't want one of your earth-shaking climaxes to dislodge it, do I?"

From the far corner, Johnson sniggered at my query, and fleetingly, I lifted my chin to meet his amused gaze.

"What do you think, doctor?" I asked. "Am I doing everything I can to meet Hilary's needs?"

"Well, she didn't get her drink, but it seems her other requirements have been well thought through, boss." He laughed harder, watching as I secured the tape in place, taping the vibrator against her sex.

"Indeed, they have," I agreed, casting a gaze down the length of her body.

Her tits still looked astonishingly good pegged by the clothespins, and there was just the faintest sign of sweat building at her brow as my nefarious plan fell into place like the pieces of a puzzle.

"The best of it is, I don't even have to be here to revel in your pleasure, Hilary." I nodded toward the corner of the room. "I have a number of perfectly placed cameras here to capture all the best bits, and your new best friend between your legs can be operated by remote control."

Throwing the tape down onto the mattress, I reached into my pocket, this time clasping the small black remote, holding it aloft for her to see. "All I have to do is use this to keep you suspended in perpetual ecstasy."

She panted around the gag, as well she might. Hilary was only just beginning to understand the predicament she'd landed in.

"A demonstration, then." I flicked on the switch, watching her hips jerk as the plastic sprung to life at her sex. "We can start gently and build up, or we can go right to factor ten, Hilary." I took a step closer, assessing her expression as I nudged up the intensity.

She moaned around the plastic, her wrists pulling futilely at the straps holding them down as though the bondage had suddenly disappeared.

"Yes," I agreed in a mocking tone. "I know that's good." Crouching by her side, I pressed down lightly on the vibrator, ensuring it sat snugly between her lips while the curved edge cradled her clit.

"Seems like she's enjoying it, Sir."

I grinned at Johnson's shrewd observation.

"Oh, yes," I cooed. "Even though she doesn't want to. Even

though she's exposed, bound, her wonderful tits pegged, and every fiber of her wants to resist, little Hilary has no choice. She's going to come for me now, then over and over until she thinks she can't take anymore."

Johnson's laughter floated past my ears, but my focus never lifted from Hilary—the allure of her chest rising and falling, the way her fingers gripped the wooden chair, and as I dragged my hungry gaze south, the way her hips rocked to the rhythm of the pulsating plastic.

"What happens then, Sir?" Johnson asked from the corner behind me. "What happens when she can't take anymore?"

Running my tongue over my teeth, I considered his question. The answer was immediate, as natural as the sunrise.

"Then I push past the threshold."

Hilary's strangled cry interrupted the pleasing thought. Running one finger along her inner thigh, I watched as her body erupted, every muscle tensed, her breath ragged. Detonating, her eyes closed, and her back arched. I smiled at the sight, my hand sweeping back to her sex to confirm what I already suspected. Beneath the vibrator was one wet pussy, and by the time I was through with her, she'd be flooded in her own hedonistic arousal.

"Good girl," I soothed, my cock swelling further at the damp fabric meeting my fingers. "That was your first orgasm."

Tilting her head in my direction, her eyes flickered open. Our gazes locked for one long moment, her hips rising sporadically as she rode the final waves of pleasure.

"What do you say, little girl?"

Hilary's gaze narrowed at my question, and I rewarded her by sliding the dial on the remote control up another ratchet.

"Ommmm."

There was no choice but to chuckle at her response. I couldn't tell what she was trying to tell me, though it seemed fairly clear it wasn't the gratitude I'd requested. Still, she was adorable and smoking hot.

Pressing my digits against her damp panties, I taunted her sex with the one thing it would badly desire, but I wouldn't permit it—anything to fill her up, anything to complete her. My fingers, my cock—she would have to wait and beg for both.

"You're welcome." I glanced back at her flustered face, lifting those same fingers to my nose and inhaling the intoxicating scent of her sex. My cock thickened on demand, though it would have to learn patience as well. Rising to my feet, I turned to Johnson. "Get me another chair in here. I'm going to watch the show for a while, then I'm hitting the sack."

"Yes, boss." He smiled, throwing one lingering glance in Hilary's direction before he sauntered from the room, and I couldn't blame him. The squirming blonde was absolutely mesmerizing to watch, and though she couldn't understand the lesson I was teaching, she would with time. Either she obeyed, or she was made to comply. Rule two was non-negotiable.

CHAPTER 9: HILARY

Darkness once more. The all-encompassing variety, the sort that threatened to swallow me up altogether. I had no idea how long I'd been here, what time of day it was, or how long the dreaded vibrator had been buzzing its relentless charm on my clit. At first, I'd kept count of the climaxes it ripped from me, finding peculiar comfort in holding onto the number. It was better than having to acknowledge what was actually happening—the dark, dank room and my most intimate parts on display, not only for the loathsome Sean but for the doctor and whoever else decided to wander in and witness my denigration. Counting helped to mute those extraneous factors—the biting clothespins, the plastic shoved between my teeth, the leather at my wrists and ankles, and worse, the unnerving knowledge, despite the pain and anguish, there was a sick, twisted part of me that was enjoying the angst. I loathed that he had bound and exposed me, but the powerlessness of not being able to prevent it or cover myself was as enticing as it was excruciating. It tapped into the same perverse psychology that had relished submitting to Saul, to the brunt of his palm as he'd spanked me, and the rub of his ropes.

Saul.

The image of my lover's face flashed before my eyelids as the damned plastic edged me back to the brink, but I pushed his face away. I couldn't handle thinking about him at the moment—how angry he'd be with me for landing myself in the sorry situation or even the things he'd do to Sean once he found out. Those considerations were for another day, a moment when I wasn't being forced into the abyss over and over. Once upon a time, I complained I didn't come often enough, but that seemed laughable in light of my current plight. My body was exhausted with the weight of the plea-sure, my muscles limp with fatigue, and still, it went on, the low thrum of the battery-operated fiend between my thighs punctuated only by my occasional muffled cries and the haunting laughter that wafted from beyond my bondage.

Sean.

Sean fucking Hyland.

He was laughing at me, amused by the pitiful situation he'd forced me into, and though I couldn't see him, I knew he was there somewhere. Seated on the fucking chair, the doctor had brought in for him, watching my desperate, debased decline. I pulled in air through my nostrils, my head fit to burst with the dichotomy. How dare he do this to me! How dare he take me and tie me up in this awful, humiliating way. What was the man trying to achieve—death by orgasm? He said he didn't intend to kill me, but why should I trust the word of a nefarious stranger? Especially one so gleeful at my denigration.

"Wonderful." His hilarity floated through the air. "You are a fucking delight."

My jaw, already aching at being compelled around the plastic ball, clenched at his assessment. There was nothing even vaguely wonderful about any of this.

"I wonder how long I can keep you this way? How much pleasure can you take before you just lose consciousness?"

My chest rose and fell, my gaze landing on the cruel wooden clothespins still clamped around my sensitive tissue. He couldn't be serious, could he? He wouldn't really just leave me like this? My clit ached from the unyielding attention from the vibrator, the impotency of my predicament weighing down on me like lead. I couldn't take much more, and however much I detested his scornful attention, the thought of being left like this alone was worse—a suffocating reality.

"Please!" I screeched the word from around the gag, though naturally, the sound came more like a string of indecipherable vowels, the resonance shaming me in spite of my already impossible position.

"What was that?" Sean's voice was louder, and as I searched the dark ceiling for the thousandth time, his face came into view. "Do you have something to say, sweetheart?"

My focus flitted to the place his voice had radiated from, a hundred responses right there on the tip of my tongue, but of course, the gag ensured none of them were possible.

"Don't look at me like that." His tone was playful, but he folded his arms across his chest, the gesture reminiscent of the man I'd bumped into in the coffee shop, igniting this whole sordid affair. "If you have something respectful you'd like to say to me, nod your head."

Arching away from the monstrous plastic beast as best I could, I nodded firmly, trying to ignore the hideous smirk which painted his face.

"Okay, then." Dropping to his haunches, his hands shifted to my face, one finger dipping under the leather strap at my face and easing the ball from my lips.

Finally liberated, I stretched my lips, swallowing hard as he continued.

"This is your chance, little girl. Talk."

"Please, Sir." I hardly registered the pleading tone coming from me or the way my toes curled at the abject humiliation. The only thing on my mind was stopping the damn vibrator —seeking a reprieve so I could think, focus, and decide how to get the hell out of here.

"Please, what?" His tone was clipped, and tension ratcheted in my body at the ominous timbre.

"Please, no more," I begged, my throat dry and sore from whatever drugs he'd pushed through my bloodstream.

"You don't like my hospitality?" he asked sardonically. "I can assure you most of the men who end up in here have more to worry about than climaxes."

"Please." The intensity between my legs was growing again, tormenting me in its unique, unyielding ability to take me higher, whether or not I sought the release. "I can't." Close to tears, I squeezed my eyes shut, unable to handle either the arrogant glint in his eyes or the looming inevitability of the sensations.

"But you're so much fun to watch." A hand at my arm drew my gaze open again, his fingers trailing a line under my pegged breast. "So delectable."

"You've had your fun now." My voice broke with the statement, the last vestment of my pride cracking with it. "Please, just stop. Just let me go."

Sean eyed me thoughtfully, and reaching into his pocket, he produced the remote control that decided my fate, sliding it between his fingers.

"I can't do that, beautiful." He ran his digit over the small plastic box, my attention fixed on the deed.

I held my breath, knowing this was all part of the game. He was playing with me, demonstrating his authority over my body as though this terrible ordeal hadn't done so already. The pressure on my clit eased, only a fraction, the plastic still vibrating happily at my weary sex, but it was enough—enough to placate me, enough to send a message he was listening and could be kind.

"Better?" His tone was sardonic, but there was no denying the inevitable. It was better, a more manageable predicament. For now, at least.

"Thank you, Sir."

He smiled. "See, I can be caring as well as cruel, and while I am not going to give you up, I don't want to see you in agony, Hilary." Placing the remote on the hard floor beside me, he edged closer, one hand reaching between my bound legs. "I only want you wet and ready for what comes next."

"You've made your point," I panted, trying desperately to resist the urge to climax again, now that the intensity of the vibrator had been reduced. "You're in charge, I get it."

His smile widened. "You're damn right, I am. I'm in charge of you, and soon, I'll be in control of this whole shitty city." His fingers brushed past the edge of the plastic, grazing my lips, soaked by the endless rounds of pleasure. "I didn't come here looking for another hot blonde, but you're one hell of a sweetener."

His hand skimmed over my aching clit until it found the tape he'd used to secure the vibrator. I gasped as he tugged it, pulling it from my flesh in one fell swoop. The relief was immediate, a reprieve for my desperate clit, but it was short-lived, the end of the vibrating monster already at my sex, and before I could process what was happening, he pushed the thing inside me.

"Fuck!" I screamed the word, yanking at the immovable binds at my wrists yet again. I didn't care what he made of my responses, whether he approved of my language or not. After so long and so many orgasms, there was no other reaction to being impaled by the pulsing plastic.

"I know." Sean's gaze swept right to my face. "I've never wanted to be a vibrator so much in my whole damn life."

"Oh, God." My eyes closed as he eased the thing from me before thrusting it deep inside again, and it was good—so fucking good. I was wet and desperate for its attention, the urge to be filled almost primal as it took its fill of me at his hand. "Please!"

"Please, what?"

His voice was louder, and by the time I opened my eyes, he was closer to me, leaning over my face even as his left hand controlled the pace at my sex.

"Please, Sir." I didn't know what I was begging for anymore. Did I want him to fuck me with the bloody thing, or did I want him to leave me the hell alone? I was so aroused by his malicious attention, the desire for his focus as shocking as it was unspoken, but it was real—a true tangible entity. As he pumped the plastic in and out of me, the wet sounds of my pussy filled my ears, reminding me of the truth.

I was enjoying this.

Whatever I said, however I chose to cope, I relished the way he denigrated me, tearing those climaxes from my clit, and now the way he was fucking me with the same awful sex toy. I should hate it, but I didn't, or I didn't only hate it. There was pleasure as well. Deep, tangible hedonism that grew at my core, burgeoning each time the vibrating monster speared me.

"Fuck, I'm going to come again."

I could scarcely catch my breath at the revelation, the admission shocking. How was this possible? How was he able to bring me back to the brink when he wasn't even touching my clit anymore? Hell, the sensitive bud was so sore, I was grateful he wasn't stimulating it, yet still, he'd been able to harness all of my need, sending me right back to the edge again.

"Not without my permission, little girl." Sean grinned at my gaping expression. "I know how good this is for you, but you've had quite enough orgasms. There'll be no more until you agree to my terms."

"No." I arched my back as much as the fucking binds would allow. "No, please!"

Even though he was right—he had taken me higher than anyone and made me climax more than even Saul—the thought of not grasping this latest high was unbearable. Whatever this was, it was something new, a hedonism I had never known before, and the looming orgasm felt deep and powerful. I couldn't give it up now. I hadn't endured all of this torment to be left wanting and unsatisfied.

"Oh, yes." He slowed the rhythm of the vibrator, smirking. "It's time you learned the most important rule, baby girl—Sean always gets his way."

I opened my mouth, panting for air as I tried to push back down on the plastic that had tempted and plagued me for so long, but it was too far away, held just out of reach of my greedy sex. I groaned with frustration as he laughed at my wanton display.

"No more, naughty girl," he mocked. "Not until you get my permission."

"Please." My attention was back on him in a heartbeat, the passion tightening inside, willing to ignore everything—my embarrassment, my humiliating debasement—just to get this one final, momentous high. "Sir, tell me what you want. I'll do anything."

Sean edged the tip back to my lips, pulsing it in and out of me, just enough to stir the gripping desire at my core, enough to give me hope. "Anything, eh?"

"Yes," I assured him, pushing my hips up in a vain attempt to garner more of the pleasure. "Anything you say. Anything you want. I promise."

This feeling was everything. This blooming pleasure, the likes of which I had never known. It was going to consume me, whatever happened, and I had to face the facts. I was either going to be overwhelmed by the intensity of the pleasure, left processing what was likely to be the greatest hedonism of my life, or I'd be left reeling with the loss, bereft at the way things ended without the soul-shaking orgasm, and still no closer to getting out of Sean's grasp.

No, that couldn't happen.

I couldn't let that happen.

If I was going to be bound in this shit show, I might as well lap up the ecstasy. I may as well devour whatever he had to offer.

"I want you, Hilary." He pushed the plastic deeper once more, and I panted at the tantalizing sensation as it stretched me, edging closer to my cervix. "Not just in this dark place, but in whatever dark place I choose to keep you."

I was vaguely aware of his other hand moving for the remote control, but before I had time to process it, the vibrator sped up again, the intensity catching me unaware and making me cry out. He fucked me with it, withdrawing the offending toy before slamming it back into me, sending electricity bursting through my body and reawakening the unsatisfied need at my core, the part of me that reveled in this depravity. The part that longed to give up control and be used like this every day—the facet that wanted to be his.

"Yes, Sir!"

It was easier to say the words, simpler to give him what he wanted because I craved them, too. Not in real life, of course. There was still a sane and sensible element of me somewhere that knew I couldn't cope with a monster like Sean in real life, but whoever that woman was, she was gagged and muted by the power of his presence. The ferocity of his control paralyzed her, just as I suspected the looming wall of pleasure would.

"I want to keep you tied and exposed." His hard, blue eyes drilled into me, drinking in my fettered body and landing on the clothespins still biting at my nipples. "I want to keep you wet and desperate for me, on the edge like this, all day and all night."

"Oh, fuck." The things he proposed sounded so good—much better than I knew they would be, much better than they should.

"I'd want more than that." His gaze widened imperceptibly as he leaned closer to my face, all the while, his left hand kept up its pace at my pussy, sliding the vibrating beast in and out of me. "This wouldn't be enough. I'd want to make it official."

God, I was close. So close. Close to this unknown quantity, to the unbridled passion I'd never known I was missing until now, to the tsunami of powerful pleasure that was going to sweep me up and take me away. I glanced up at him, my lips parted as I tried to focus on his face, on his words... but nothing made sense anymore.

Nothing was clear.

"Do you understand me, Hilary?" Sean's grin grew, an ominous sign my brain, fogged with arousal, barely even noticed. "You'd be mine. Not just like this. Not only in the eyes of my men, and that idiot, Morrison, but in the eyes of God as well."

The buzz of the vibrator intensified again, making all legible thoughts impossible. I was fucked. Not just by the onerous plastic in my snatch or even by the evil genius in charge of it, who played my body like an instrument, but by my own base needs for more—more of his time, more of his sadistic attention, and more of this unbelievable pleasure. It was too damned much.

"Hilary." His growl drew my focus back to the present, to the blue gaze searing into me, and to the way the pace of the plastic had increased, the thing screwing me harder and faster than before. "Did you hear me? I'm going to make you my wife."

I saw his lips moving, and from somewhere distant in my mind, the words echoed, but they were meaningless, useless. Devoid of all significance as the world became a smaller, more oppressive place. A place where the only thing that mattered was the well of sensation about to be unleashed and my ability to dive into it.

"Yes, Sir." I closed my eyes, throwing my head back against the unrelenting chair. Fuck the things he needed. Fuck the fetters at my wrists, and whoever else was here to witness my disgrace—I didn't care anymore. I only wanted this feeling—to swim in it, swallowed up by it. "Yes, Sir... anything."

The last conscious thought that flitted through my mind before the black serenity engulfed me wasn't of Sean or even the troublesome plastic he'd used to virtually destroy me—it was of Saul. The man I'd been fucking for the last few weeks. The man I'd trusted. The man I thought I knew. In all that time, however good I'd thought the sex had been, Saul had never made me feel this way. He'd never even come close.

This was the best I'd ever known.

CHAPTER 10: SEAN

Marriage. The idea was preposterous. Reprehensible in any other context, but now, watching as Hilary detonated around the vibrating plastic, it made an odd sort of sense. I'd been looking for a long-term girlfriend back in France for a while but hadn't found anyone to my liking. French women were exotic and intriguing, but when push had come to shove, I rarely wanted to stay with any of them. They looked charming on my arm for a few weeks, but I tired of them, seeking the next dalliance to replace the thrill. I needed something longer-lasting, someone who engaged my brain as well as my cock, and the tempting feisty Hilary might well be that woman. Of course, that was still a nonsensical argument for matrimony. Why even consider such a twisted arrangement in my position? Zander never got married—no men in my position seemed to. Marriage was about real commitment, and the type of devotion usually discarded in the upper echelons of mob gangs. In my business, women were like commodities—shipped in to entertain and please, look pretty, but for no deeper reasons.

I exhaled, my cock swelling as Hilary spasmed again, her limbs tense and mouth stretched wide to accommodate the weight of sensation. Eyeing her parted lips, I imagined slipping my length between them and the exquisite feel of her hot, silky throat as it enveloped me. The image bloomed in my mind until it consumed me, making me catch my breath. I would have that pleasure… soon. I'd fuck every hole she had to offer to reinforce the lesson I'd just taught, yet the idea of making the arrangement permanent goaded.

What would marriage to a woman like Hilary be like? I was giddy at the concept of her devotion—she was literally everything I'd fantasized about—beautiful, yes, but strong-willed as well, with a keen eye and a smart mouth to match. She would likely also know about my lifestyle. Working for Morrison would have exposed her, though that said, she'd been fabulously naïve in the face of my menace. The most tempting aspect of the writhing blonde, though, wasn't her aesthetics or whether or not she was switched on—it was the way she'd responded to my torment.

Yes, she had come because the vibrator demanded it, but it had been more than that. Her soaked cunt was evidence of how much the experience had affected her. Hilary hadn't just experienced superficial orgasms, she'd come alive as my hostage, and the climax she was now enjoying looked to be one of the most significant I'd ever ripped from another person's body. I could have more than just fun with a woman like that. I could spend a lifetime unpicking her triggers and using them to captivate her.

"Fuck."

She whispered the word as I eased the vibrator from her, holding the plastic up to examine it while she continued to jerk and moan below me. As suspected, the toy was drenched with her arousal. Bringing it to my nostrils, I inhaled the scent of her glorious sex, my balls aching at the taunting aroma.

I wanted her, and not just now in this shitty interrogation space, but in my bed, on my cock... at my feet. Glancing down at her flushed face, I considered the conundrum. I could have all those things with the right level of coercion, could make her agree to anything—this little fray had proven that. She'd kneel, beg, and sing if I ordered it, but something that would usually set me on fire about the thought was missing. Some key feature failed to ignite. I didn't want to just beat Hilary into submission, I wanted to bait her into it, keep some of the mettle I'd seen demonstrated so wonderfully in the coffee shop, alongside this new wet, subservient version. Why choose one when I could have both? The very best of it was if I kept her, and God forbid, if I married her, it would be the sweetest two fingers in the world to that arrogant son of a bitch, Morrison—a constant, nagging reminder to him that he had lost, not just Hilary, but the city. I would swallow up every inch of Zander's original territory, then I'd come for Saul's patch—for him. Morrison was old and getting slow while I was more dynamic. Life on the continent had taught me a trick or two, and I was prepared to play any card to get what I wanted. Right now, that meant revenge for Zander's murder, a ring on Hilary's finger, and a collar around her neck.

Smiling at the thought, I flicked the vibrator off, turning my attention back to the dazed woman still tied to the chair.

"How was that, darling?"

"Oh, God." She inhaled, her eyes falling closed. "I've never, ever known anything like it."

"Good." I rounded the back of the chair, and bracing, lifted it back to its feet, righting Hilary on the way. "That's just how I want things to be for you, sweetheart. Better than ever." I whispered the words into her nape, resisting the urge to drag my lips across the perfumed skin. "And all you have to do is everything I tell you."

She twisted her head to try to meet my eyes. "Sean? Sir?"

"Mmmm?" I like the way she said that. My name sounded better on her lips than a thousand women before her.

"What is it you want?"

I chuckled into her soft flesh, rising to tower over her once again.

"I already told you, beautiful. Weren't you paying attention?"

Naturally, that wasn't fair. I had some idea how distracted by pleasure Hilary had been when I'd laid out the terms of her orgasm, but it made no difference. In all the years I'd been rolling the dice, there had been no evidence life was fair and little prospect of that changing now.

"I'm sorry, Sir." Her face fell, a sign perhaps of genuine contrition on her part.

Unthinkingly, I leaned lower, snaking my arms around her chest to the place my wooden pegs were still jutting out proudly. Fuck, they looked great on her tits, making the firm mounds all the more alluring, but I knew she'd worn them for a long time, and her nipples would need a rest. Without overthinking the deed, I squeezed the arms of both pegs at the same time, releasing the pressure and slipping them into my inside pocket.

"Fffff..." She released the hurt with gritted teeth, but I was pleased she hadn't felt the need to resort to profanity again. Obscenities during climax were understandable, but I couldn't excuse it at all costs.

"Good girl." My hands slid back to her breasts again, massaging the wonderful assets while she panted in response. "I know you need to let go sometimes, but I would prefer fewer cuss words from these pretty lips."

I lifted my head to find Johnson still there, smirking at Hilary. He'd been there the whole time, despite my initial instruction, standing in the corner, along with whoever else had come and gone while I taunted her. Johnson would reiterate, he was there for her safety, but it was obvious he was hot for my new acquisition, desperate to taste the woman I wanted to claim as mine. My brows furrowed at the idea. I'd never been shy about sharing women before nor about showing them off, and I wasn't sorry I'd displayed Hilary this time—I could tell the shame had magnified her senses—but all of a sudden, the idea of him just standing there, watching, irked me. I'd already told him to leave us—why hadn't he gone?

"You're dismissed, Johnson."

His body straightened. "But Sir, what if she has a bad reaction to the sedative?"

Kneading her tits, I fixed him with a hard stare.

"You told me we were past the point of concern."

"Well, yes, Sir." He shifted his weight awkwardly. "We probably are, but—"

"So, I will contact you if I need you." I determined there and then, I would never call on Johnson again. He had seen far too much of Hilary for my liking. I would find another doctor. Like everything, they were a dime a dozen in my world.

"Yes, Sir." He looked crestfallen as he shuffled toward the door, offering one final furtive glance Hilary's way before he departed.

"And then, there were two." I left her glorious tits with some reluctance, coming to stand in front of her. "Do you remember what I told you I was going to do with you?"

Hilary's eyes widened at my question, her breathing accelerating.

"Not really, Sir."

I smirked, hardly surprised, based on how intense the session must have been for her.

"How disappointing." I feigned the despondency, ensuring my expression was even as I delivered it. "I'm going to need my future wife to have better focus."

That got her attention, her head snapping up to meet my gaze.

"Wife?"

My lips twitched at the stunned defiance in her voice. All it had taken was the wave of hedonism to pass and the clothespins to have been removed, and she was back—the Hilary who'd first ran into me, the one who'd piqued my interest all those hours ago.

"You're not serious? We can't get…" She paused, as though the next word had conjured a bitter taste in her mouth. "Married!"

"What was that?" I snapped, enjoying the way she recoiled at my vicious tone. "How do you speak to me, little girl?"

"Sir." She added the title I craved in an instant, the show of submission lengthening my cock even greater than I believed was possible. "We can't get married, Sir."

"Oh, but we will."

My mind was made up. I would take the woman I wanted and mold her into the perfect little plaything. I would teach her precisely how to love and honor, but most of all, she would learn deference and how to obey. At that moment, nothing else mattered, not the social fall out or the financials —none of it. After all, I had one of the best legal teams in the world. They could draft me a suitable pre-nuptial agreement, which would ensure the panting little blonde before me never got access to my huge fortune, and what else was there to worry about? I didn't care what anyone else said—I never had. The men in London who'd been loyal to my uncle would either vow the same allegiance to me or face the consequences. That was how this business worked, and they all knew it.

"We will, and you'll become Mrs. Sean Hyland." I smiled at how that sounded, the idea scintillating for the first time. "You'll be mine to have and to hold." I moved closer, propping my finger under her chin and lifting it to meet my gaze. "To bind, to expose, and to fuck, for as long as I decide."

A flicker of fear danced in her emotive eyes. "That's crazy," she gasped. "We can't get married, and you can't make me."

"That's just where you're wrong, darling," I reminded her, my thumb and forefinger tightening on her chin. "I absolutely fucking can."

CHAPTER 11: HILARY

My mind reeled as he unfastened the leather at my wrists. My initial instinct to reach out and slap the bastard who had put me through such a perturbing experience was overawed with the weight of the sensations, my emotions lurching from relief to satiation, back to rage at the treatment. The guy was talking about marriage, about making a lifelong commitment, when we'd only known each other five minutes, and in that time, he'd drugged, snatched, and done all this to me! It didn't seem comprehensible, but then based on the things I knew about the Hyland's, Sean seemed to fit the bill.

Yes, he was strikingly attractive, and something about his domineering character made me melt inside, but clearly, he was mentally unbalanced. You couldn't just meet someone and capture them as your own—it wasn't right—though even as the thoughts registered, something about the way Saul's long-term friend, Connor Reilly, had met his girlfriend, Molly, rang a bell in my mind. I didn't know the whole story, of course, seeing how I was only Saul's assistant, and my relationship with Connor had been brief at best, but I'd heard the rumors and had a good idea the way Molly had come into his life had been anything but conventional. I also knew what Connor had been charged with when they'd arrested him and the long hours of counseling Molly had undergone. To the entire world, their attraction seemed like Stockholm syndrome. I scoffed at it on more than one occasion, yet now look at my predicament—*I* was the one kidnapped, stripped, and held under duress, and now, my captor was bandying the idea of matrimony around like a second date.

"Remember what I told you." His voice was a low snarl. "Behave yourself, or I will make you regret it."

Our gazes locked for a moment, his blue eyes cold as they glowered. Right on cue, I shivered, suddenly cold now the excitement of the last climax had withered.

"You really want to marry me, Sir?" I sounded monotonic as I asked, a part of my brain still unable to comprehend the conundrum as I glanced around the disgusting room that had become my cell.

Marriage, for God's sake. I didn't even know if I wanted those things with Saul, let alone a madman I'd literally stumbled into. The last thing I needed was to bind myself to the psychopath in any meaningful way. I needed to get away, back to Saul and The Syndicate, as soon as I could. I needed to—

"Yes." The assuredness in his tone broke my train of thought, and I lifted my chin to meet his eyes again. "Yes, I do."

"But why?" It was a good question. "You could have anyone you wanted, Sir. Why me?"

I hoped stroking his ego a little, I could win his favor, and based on the way his lips curled, my ploy seemed to be working.

"I didn't know what I was missing until I found you."

He winked like something out of one of those cheesy romantic movies, but even though my heart raced at the gesture, my head knew better. This was not a movie, and there wouldn't be a happy ending. Terrible things happened to women who were captured by the enemy, and that's what Sean was. He was the one who'd inherit the Hyland empire. He'd come back to take over what his uncle had left, and apparently, me as well. My muscles tightened at the suffocating thought. I could fight all I wanted, but I'd been around The Syndicate long enough to know how these things went. Powerful men like Hyland had virtual impunity from the law. They took what they wanted, and nine times out of ten, they got away with it. My insides clenched at the insidious truth. Things were not looking good for my future.

He shifted to my ankles, and once again, I considered kicking the son of a bitch and heading for the door, but insecurity wracked my brain. I knew these buildings well enough to know there would be armed men around the place. I was half-naked and had nothing to defend myself with. Now was hardly the ideal time to launch an offensive.

But there might not be a better one, the small nagging voice in my head goaded. *This might be all the time you have left.*

"What if I don't want to marry you?" There was steel in my tone, despite its quiet volume. Liberating the final ankle strap, he met my insistent gaze.

"You'll come around to the idea."

He sounded so sure of himself, so smug and self-aware, for a moment, the rage simmering at my captivity and treatment bubbled violently, threatening to consume me. How dare he make these assumptions? How dare he think he could decide anything for me? Sean didn't know me, and what little I knew of him was cruel and odious.

"Don't do that."

I swallowed at the instruction, my brow furrowing.

"What?" I glanced around, aware I was breathing hard again as the list of accusations about him grew in my head. "Don't do what, Sir?"

It pained me to refer to him that way again. Now the fogged arousal had lifted, it was much more difficult to look the man in the eyes and infer he was in any way better than me, but at the same time, I couldn't deny how sexy it was. Every time I used the title, I was aware of how my body responded—the rush of moisture between my legs and the disturbing way my nipples, so recently abused by the wooden clothespins, beaded. It was disconcerting, to say the least, made all the worse by the fact there was nowhere for me to go—nowhere to hide from the way my body betrayed my true feelings.

"Don't look at me that way." He scowled, rising to his full height. "I can see the way your jaw clenches and your hands ball into fists but don't even think about it, Hilary. You're too fragile and hopelessly outnumbered, and let me assure you, you won't like me if you do something stupid."

Frowning, I lifted my chin in defiance. "What makes you think I like you now, *Sir*?"

That time, the title had a sardonic air, and I regretted the tone as soon as it left my lips, his narrowing blue eyes and thunderous expression flashing me a warning.

"Oh, I don't know," he said coldly. "Perhaps the enormity of the pleasure I've bestowed on you since you arrived. Save for a couple of clothespins, I haven't caused you pain, but that can all change in a heartbeat, Hilary."

He took a step back, reaching for my left wrist at the same time, dragging me out of the chair. I fell forward, stumbling in his direction, perilously aware just how naked and vulnerable I was as I brushed against his body.

"Turn around." His expression was serious as he gave the order, his right hand signaling for me to spin and face the other direction. It took every ounce of my willpower not to come back with my usual sarcastic type of retort—a witticism about how he could turn around if he wanted to, but I was just fine here. My heart pounded even faster, thanks to the brooding look in his eyes, which persuaded me it would be better to keep my mouth closed and, for once, just do as I was told.

Pulling in a shaky breath, I turned, my feet cold against the hard floor in only my pantyhose. Standing in the direction he wanted me, I waited, my senses waiting for something—a strike of pain perhaps or another instruction. Inevitably, the bastard made me wait, and it seemed to take forever, standing there in the shadows with only the sound of my hammering heart and the rhythm of his breath at my shoulder.

"Hands behind your back."

As soon as the command came, I knew, with a sinking heart, what it meant—he wanted to bind me again, and this time, he'd ensure my hands were secured behind me. There was a spike of frustrated fear as my wrists slid into position, an odd acceptance of my fate, even though I knew it was inevitable, and everything I had already summated was true. I wouldn't get away easily. He was too big for me. The place would be crawling with armed men. I was half-naked. Though, as I felt the metal slide across my flesh, none of those excuses seemed to justify my resigned compliance.

I could do better than this, couldn't I? Saul would expect me to fight back, wouldn't he?

It was too late, and as I heard the metal click into place, a spike of terror rose from my belly. Sean Hyland had just cuffed me, and God only knew what awaited me next.

"Good girl, Hilary." His breath was hot against the side of my neck, his tone mocking, but I forced myself to ignore the chiding tone. Sean had cuffed me and demanded not only my capitulation but that I become his wife. However much I loathed the proposition, I needed him in a very tangible way, and if I ever wanted to get out of these cuffs and out of Hyland's network, I'd have to stay in his good books—for the time being, at least. "I knew you could be obedient if you tried."

I turned my head at the sound of his voice, half tantalized, half disturbed.

Who was this man?

I knew who he was, of course—the long-lost nephew of Zander Hyland—but what was it about me he found so fascinating, and what emotions was it I saw burning in those deep blue eyes?

"I'm scared, Sean." I risked the confession as his hand slid to the small of my back and guided me toward the door. I was moving toward the object I'd sought the entire time he'd had me tied up here, yet as it approached, the exit loomed with nothing but trepidation. Anything could be on the other side of that door—anything and anyone—and I was still practically naked, breasts jutting out from the underwiring of my defaced bra, my ass on display, save for the tiny thong panties I'd donned at the beginning of the day for Saul.

"Don't forget your manners." Stepping in front of me, he halted my progress, but there was a dark twinkle in his eyes as he responded to my plea.

"I'm sorry, Sir." I gulped at the intensity radiating from him, uncertain if it boded well for me. Yes, he had taken me, but it was also true, he hadn't permitted any actual harm to happen unless you counted the damage to my clothing.

"Tell me about your fear." His tone was soft yet demanding, the resonance almost hypnotic as one hand guided me closer to him, and the other caught under my chin.

Some sane part of my brain wanted to laugh. Tell him about it? Tell him about the terror he had inspired—the whole thing was laughable—but I didn't chuckle. In fact, I had rarely felt so serious as I absorbed his thoughtful expression. He seemed solemn, genuinely interested in the things that concerned me.

"Being like this." I gestured down to my exposed chest. "Anyone could see me when we leave here, Sir."

His lips twitched, and for one awful moment, I wondered just what he had in store for me.

"That's the point, beautiful." He trailed one finger along the flesh of my jaw. "I want everyone to see you. I want my men to know the prize I have claimed is not only wonderful but entirely off-limits."

My lips parted, though, for a moment, there were no words as the realization of that statement washed over me.

"You want them to see me?"

"Yes." He smiled. "Every fabulous inch of you that's on display is there for them to ogle. They can look but never touch. You belong to the boss man now."

CHAPTER 12: SEAN

The look on her face was priceless, worth more than any diamonds or the overpriced artwork strewn on my walls in Nice. There was a flicker of disgust, a response perhaps to the way I viewed her as my property, though that was something little Hilary would have to get used to. Beyond that glimmer, though, there was something else—an unspoken yearning she couldn't tell me about. Maybe she hadn't recognized it herself until this very moment, but it was there in her wide-eyed gaze.

"You have no choice but to trust me." I stroked the side of her heated cheek, wondering how I'd stumbled into someone so beautiful—so perfect for my wants and needs. I'd always been a lucky son of a bitch, and Hilary only proved just how much. I pressed her closer to my body until her swollen nipples grazed my shirt. "I can be a mean bastard, but I'm not bad to the core."

She pulled her lower lip between her teeth, apparently uncertain.

"I-I don't know what to say," she stammered. "One minute, I was living my life, and now this…" Her gaze traveled around the dark space I'd held her in before returning to me. "And now you say I have to marry you?"

I could hear the edge of defiance in her tone and how hard she fought to resist it. It made me almost proud, knowing she'd tried.

"Remember my second rule?" I arched an eyebrow.

"Y-Yes, Sir."

"What was it?" I towered over her, expectant at her prompt and polite reply.

"That I should obey you."

"Exactly." Nodding, I allowed myself to smile. She had been paying attention and did recall. "What I need from you right now—*all* I need from you—is your obedience and trust. In my experience, one is derived from the other."

"But I don't know you." Her brows knitted with her emphatic tone. "You're just some guy from the coffee shop, Sir."

I chuckled at her reasoning. Logical it may have been, but it was irrelevant to Hilary at this juncture.

"Not to you," I corrected. "Not anymore. I am the most important person in the world. The man who decides where you are and what happens to you there. The one who will decide whether to expose or clothe you. The one who you will look to for everything."

She panted as I laid out her fate.

"And it doesn't matter what I think about any of it, Sir?" Her shoulders squared back, fury flickering in her eyes. "It doesn't matter if I don't want you, don't want to marry you?"

"No, it doesn't matter." Only her inclusion of my title and her barely polite tone had saved her from experiencing one of my legendary punishments right here, right now. I had a reputation for my no-nonsense approach to both work and play, and Hilary was going to have to toe the line if she didn't want to learn that lesson. So far, I had been kind, but I could be callous. "You will come around to my way of thinking in the end, and if you behave, I will make sure your compliance is well rewarded."

"Like today?" She twisted to glance back at the chair she had been bound to. "Is that what my compliance will buy me?"

My hand rose into her honeyed locks, my fingers tightening as I drew her focus back in my direction.

"You only get one warning, little girl, and this is it." My voice was a deep growl, and her eyes widened like teacups. "That attitude and tone will not get you anywhere with me, so whatever you've learned in your life about how to behave, you need to unlearn. I am not some wishy-washy guy like Saul Morrison. I'm a Hyland, and I will not stand for your bullshit."

"O-Okay, I'm sorry, Sir." There was genuine terror in her voice, its tone shaky as she realized the gravity of her situation. She wasn't only half-naked and bound, she was also pissing off the only person who could offer her protection from the mauling grasp of the men outside, and I had no doubt they would claw to get their mitts on flesh as wonderful as hers. "I just..." she hesitated, her gaze falling as far as my fist would allow.

"What?" I demanded. "You just what?"

She pulled in a quivering breath, and I took a moment to enjoy the look of her goosing flesh, the way her nipples beaded into tight little knots, and her flushed expression.

"I didn't expect this." She appealed to me with those large, imploring eyes. "I still don't know what's going to happen to me, Sir. I'm..." She bit her lower lip, evidently torn about what to say next.

"Go on," I coaxed.

"I'm afraid," she barely whispered. "I know what happens to women who get taken by groups like yours. I don't want to end up like that."

Something about her candor spoke to me in a way I rarely experienced. I heard men begging for their lives with dull regularity. Rivals and fools who thought they could play me who always lost, but rarely had I heard such an honest admission from a woman as wonderful as Hilary, and for some reason, her plea worked. It tugged at my heartstrings and made me want to comfort her.

"You'll be okay." I released the fist in her hair, cradling the sides of her face. "If you're a good girl and do as I say, you'll be fine. No one else will touch you, and I will treat you well."

She batted her lashes at me, her train of thought obvious, even though she was sensible enough not to vocalize it. *I would treat her well?* The same man who had drugged, bound, and stripped her for mere sport—*I* was going to do that?

"Yes, me." I smiled as I answered her unspoken query. "I'm not always a cruel guy, Hilary. I'm just misunderstood."

Her lips twitched at that, but the evident terror in her body refused to allow it to morph into more.

"Misunderstood, Sir?"

"That's right." Slipping my hands around her body, I held her against me, and for the first time, I noticed how cold she'd become. It was time to wrap this up and get her to my room. "I won't ever raise my hand to you in anger or fuck you against your will." I squeezed the perfect orbs of her arse. "But I will take what belongs to me, Hilary, and right now, that's you."

"Now and forever, Sir." She murmured the words into my collar bone.

"What?" I drew back, lifting her chin to hear her more clearly. "What was that?"

"If we get married, it won't just be for now." She shrugged as far as the cuffs would allow. "I would be your wife forever unless you planned to divorce me."

"Is that what's worrying you?" I glanced at her concerned expression and sniggered. It seemed Hilary had the weight of all the world's troubles on her slim shoulders. If I achieved nothing else with my venture, I would help alleviate that burden. I didn't know what life had been like as Hyland's squeeze, but now she was mine, she didn't have to worry about anything. I would take care of her. I would take care of it all.

"I have no plans to divorce you," I assured her. "I'm a serious man, Hilary, and I don't mention marriage lightly. You will be my wife and have all the respect that comes with that position. We just have to be clear. I am the one who makes the rules in the marriage. You will still call me Sir, and I will still expect your obedience."

She gulped at my verdict, and it seemed as though a battle raged inside her. There was clearly a side of Hilary that relished the idea of subservience to me. I had witnessed that when I'd brought her to her soul-shattering climax earlier, but I wasn't a fool. There were also other parts of her that still wanted to resist—to spit in my face and flee—and those parts needed managing.

"And what will I do, Sir?" She tilted her head to meet my eyes. "What will I do if I become your wife?"

"Whatever I tell you." I grinned at that thought, imaging her bound and semi-naked by my desk every day.

"I'm serious." Her jaw tightened, and I half expected her to stamp her foot like an irate schoolgirl. "What will I do with my life?"

"We'll find something for you," I soothed, sensing I needed to iron out these creases in her concerns. "But in the short term, your focus will be on me. On pleasing me, on making me happy."

"Sex, you mean?" She searched my face, I assumed for some sign of ill-intent. "I thought you weren't going to force yourself on me."

"No, not just sex," I lied, though my cock swelled in my pants at the alluring imagery playing out in my head. "And I meant what I said, Hilary. I won't take you by force."

"So, if I refuse, you'll respect that, Sir?"

I bit back on the small snicker that threatened to rise at her plaintive comment.

"Oh, you won't refuse me, sweetheart. By the time I'm finished with you, you'll be purring like a pussy cat, begging for my cock."

Her brow furrowed, but before she could offer a smart-arse reply, I reached for the gag still hanging around her neck.

"Let me help you," I murmured, easing the ball and strap back into place. "Let me stop that pretty little tongue before it gets you into trouble."

"No, please, Sean!" She pulled against the cuffs, trying to twist out of my embrace, but the hand on her delicious back-side grabbed the metal at her wrists and held her in place with comparative ease, ignoring the way her feet sought to retreat. "I'll be good. I'll be quiet!" She was turning her head side to side in a vain attempt to defy me, but it was hopeless. The leather strap was already in the right position at the back of her head, and with a practiced hand, I lifted the plastic ball into place just in time to cut off her latest impassioned plea.

This time she did stamp her feet, scowling at me as the

consonants continued to try to bleed from her tempting lips. Leaning closer, I ran my hand through her hair, eventually pulling the length back roughly.

"Behave yourself," I reminded her with a playful snarl. "Remember what happens to naughty girls who piss me off. I can protect you from the rabid mob and still have a little fun at your expense." My brow rose at the threat, and right on cue, she started to pant around the ball gag. "All you have to do is be good. Walk when I tell you to walk. Stop when I tell you to stop. Look smoking hot and blush when all those hungry male eyes crawl over your skin."

Her eyes widened at my inference, a desperate mewl escaping her gagged mouth.

"Exactly." I cajoled. "You can do all those things for me and survive, can't you, sweetheart?"

Releasing her hair, I pinched one, then the other tantalizing nipple, reveling in the way she fought for composure. Hilary might have been afraid, but there was more than terror going on in her sweet head. There was good old-fashioned lust as well. That was her Achilles heel, as far as I could see. She might want her freedom, but she'd learn to desire the things I could give her even more.

CHAPTER 13: HILARY

It was impossible to say what was going through my mind as he drew away. My head was spinning, the intensity of his fervor merging with all my frustrated fears to make me giddy, but the bloody gag meant I couldn't even protest or let him know what I was feeling. My breathing was ragged as he pulled the door open, that slit of light I had previously longed for only heightening the ricocheting tension in my body. He was going to make me do this! He was going to make me walk from this room in only my panties and pantyhose in front of God knows who, and he was only doing it for kicks—to show me who was the boss and hammer home the point to any of the horrible men who worked for his organization that I was somehow his property. His to keep tied in here. His to degrade. His to display. Panic spiraled at the thought, but it was too late—too late to placate him, too late to plead my case, and far too late to get away. I dismissed the notion I might not even want to. Surely, that was folly. However deep and alluring his eyes were, how enticing his words could be, his actions spoke of his true intent, of the man who had captured me.

I might have been Saul's girl when I'd awoken in his expensive pad this morning, yesterday morning, or whenever the hell that was, but I was somebody else now—a woman cuffed and terribly vulnerable.

"Come on."

Sean turned back to meet my gaze, tilting his head to indicate I should follow, and against all my better impulses, I stumbled forward. I had no choice but to obey him, an image of what he might do to me if I refused surfacing in my head as I reached his shoulder. But my forced circumstances didn't mean I had to fucking like it. I didn't approve of the way he was treating me, and I didn't appreciate it. He might be able to keep me here, but Saul would find me. I had seen the way The Syndicate had tracked down its people before, and one thing was for certain, *I was* one of its people. I remembered the way Dalton and the others had found his girlfriend, Delilah, when Dalton had been in trouble with Sean's dead uncle. They were rabid in their dedication to the cause, and there was no way Saul would give up on me. Not once he'd figured out what had happened. Not once he—

"I need your attention."

I blinked, his words puncturing my internal thought process like a pin to a balloon as I turned my head in his direction. I hated not being able to speak, and the way I knew the plastic ball shoved between my teeth looked, but there was nothing I could do about that. The cuffs meant I was powerless to prevent its intrusion, just as I was helpless to stop the way everyone we met would stare at my exposed breasts. I would just have to bear that burden, tolerate the intensity of the humiliation, and pray to God, it didn't arouse me the way it had before. I definitely couldn't dwell on that now.

"Good." He slid one hand around my left arm and led me

out the doorway, the change in lighting making me flinch before the new landscape came into view.

We turned left, Sean leading the way, and as my eyes adjusted, I finally took in the scenery, not that there was much to see. We were in a long corridor lined with the doors to cells presumably similar to the one I'd been held in. The dirty walls reached high on either side, but there was little in the way of natural light on offer. That was probably a reprieve, based on the smell of the place, and as I scuttled to keep up with his long strides, I tried not to think about what might be dried all over the walls we passed. It took a few moments to reach the end of the dank hallway, each moment laced with paranoia, someone could come out of one of those doors and see me, but as we approached, the metal doors of an elevator slid open in front of us.

"In we go."

I let him guide me in with no resistance. The floor in the cubicle looked decidedly cleaner than the ground I'd just been walking on, but as I stepped inside, I was greeted with the mirrored image of my own reflection on all three sides of the unit. Panting, I absorbed the look of the woman staring back at me. Her blonde hair was a bedraggled mess, hemmed in by the black leather strap wound around it, securing the plastic ball into place at her mouth. My eyes lingered over the thing, taking in the way my lips were stretched wide. It was every inch as excruciating as I'd imagined in my head, my inability to communicate only exacerbated by its prominent look. Its message was clear—the woman wearing it was not permitted to speak. She didn't get to decide when to do that anymore—those things were above her paygrade—but worse was the rush of desire that tugged keenly at my core as I registered the thought. I liked it. God help me, there was something about the look and the objective of the thing I really craved, though I'd never admit such a thing to Sean.

I caught his smirking expression in his reflection behind me, and when he turned to hit the appropriate button on the control panel, I dragged my gaze over the rest of me. The first and most obvious thing that hit me were my breasts. Naturally, I'd been aware he'd cut the front away from my blouse and bra, but seeing the results for myself was something else. I looked like a sex victim, left strewn at the roadside, the jagged lines of his scissors still evident around the remaining fabric that framed my breasts. Except I was no victim, was I? What kind of prey would thoroughly enjoy their captivity as I had done? What kind would still be wet with the excitement of the orgasms he'd torn from my body? I lowered my head with shame, catching sight of my nipples and noticing how, even now, they still budded at my predicament. My body was alive with my captivity, heightened by the mortifying things he had done, even if my other senses were not.

"Turn around."

My gaze shifted at the order, catching sight of his knowing expression, but I complied regardless, hardly in a position to argue.

"You look lovely," he assured me in a sardonic tone. "No need for further appraisal on your part. Needless to say, I'll get you beautifully preened in time for our nuptials."

He was still going on about that then, was he? This incessant fascination with marriage and the absurd idea I might want to legally bind myself to him might be amusing if I hadn't been the one fettered in the arrangement. I had no desire to marry the man, and I'd be damned if I was going to let him compel me into the union. The sexual ecstasy was one thing but committing the rest of my life to him was quite another. I wouldn't be marrying anyone, and unless the British laws had changed in the matter, there wasn't anything he could do about it. Sean needed my consent, but more than that, he also needed me to sign the appropriate paperwork. I'd already decided he would get neither.

"It will get easier." He closed the distance between us with one stride, forcing me to crane my neck to meet his eyes. Damn it, had he always been this tall, or had he just kept me bound in a dark room until now? "This thing between us, this push and pull you're trying to fight."

His smile was almost wistful, one of his fingers trailing a gentle line across my cheek as the elevator lurched into action. I lowered my gaze, suddenly unable to meet the ferocity of feeling there. What did he expect me to say to that? But then, with the gag in place, there was nothing I could say, was there? Perhaps that was the point. This was the lesson he wanted to reinforce.

"I will make it good for you, Hilary." There was a flicker of emotion in his gaze, though God knows I couldn't hope to decipher it as I glanced back to meet those burning blue eyes. "I'll take what I want, the way I always do, but I want it to be good for you, too." He paused, leaning closer, and for one heart-stopping moment, I thought he was going to kiss me, but how could he with the blasted plastic in place. "One day, when all this shit has been cleaned up, I'll take you back to Nice. I think you'll really like it there, the chateaus, the champagne, and the sunshine."

What was this? Was he flirting with me—with the woman he had gagged, bound, and forced to climax to within an inch of her life?

"We'll have a good life together." His lips curled. "If we're lucky, we might even make each other happy."

I exhaled through my nostrils, uncertain how I'd respond to that ludicrous evaluation even if I could.

"But first we have to get through this episode." He glanced around as the elevator chimed to indicate we'd reached his desired floor. My insides churned, the realization we'd arrived at wherever he wanted to show me off blooming within me. "I have to tidy up the streets my uncle vacated and deal with The Syndicate, but then, you'd know all about that, wouldn't you, gorgeous?" He winked at me before grabbing my arm again and spinning me around just as the metal doors slid open.

There was little time to muse this latest twist. Sean marched from the elevator, pulling me along with him into another corridor. It was still dark, just like the basement area I'd obviously been contained in, but the ambiance here was different. The floor was polished wood, my pantyhose sliding across it as he strode off, taking me with him, and the place had an executive feel. It wasn't until we got closer, I noticed the two strapping guys waiting at the double doors beyond. No doubt they'd noticed me, though, their nefarious grins and the sickening wolf whistles evidence of that, as was the way their jaws dropped as Sean presented me.

"Good day, Mr. Hyland." The hulking blond actually licked his lips at the sight of me. "Is she a little gift for our service?"

I recoiled at the statement as far as Sean's grasp would allow, but his fingers tightened, holding me firmly in place.

"No." His tone was emphatic. "Hilary is mine."

"So, what's with the show, boss?" The other one with the receding hairline asked, though his stare never left my breasts. "Not that I'm complaining or anything, but it's just unusual. Your uncle preferred to keep his women private."

"I'm not my uncle." Sean's arms snaked to my waist,

pulling me closer. "Hilary belongs to me, but it's important she learns what that means, and if I want to display her, I will."

I squirmed at his side, my face burning with embarrassment as the two men exchanged grins.

"We're definitely happy to support you in that venture, Sir," the blond retorted. "Anything else you'll need for now?"

Sean glanced at him before his attention returned to me.

"No." His lips curled with the reply. "I think I have everything I need for the time being."

CHAPTER 14: SEAN

I whisked her into the office, regretting the decision almost immediately. I loathed everything about this place. It was Zander's signature all over the wood walls, not mine. The place was so smoke-stained and dated, it made me cringe, and that was before I contemplated the fact this was the precise place my uncle had been shot dead. My stomach churned, but I pushed the grief and anger down. I had something better to focus on, and she needed my full attention, despite the less than pleasing aesthetic of the environment.

"Stand in the middle of the room." I barked, enjoying the way she scuttled into position while my gaze took in the look of her pert backside. I hadn't had much opportunity to play with that delicious derriere yet, but I hoped there would be plenty of them coming. Chances to feel her, to squeeze her, and when she spoke out of line, which I knew she would, to turn her over my lap and tan that beautiful behind. "Good."

I closed the door, turning to watch her for a moment. Was this really the same shrill woman who'd spilled coffee on me when I'd first arrived? That smart-mouthed little kitten was difficult to decipher from the messy, shell-shocked woman trembling in front of me, though I much preferred the way she was exposed and available to me now. I'd been hard for her for fucking hours, my arousal unbearable since that final orgasm I'd ripped from her had radiated between us. I still could sense it, still see her there, bound and quivering, her body spent and desperate for more. I could smell her arousal as keenly as I felt mine, her need to be dominated, oozing from her as deeply as my craving to take control. She was fucking incredible, and I was insatiable for her.

Eyeing her perfectly formed backside, I straightened my erection inside my pants. The things I was going to do to that fine arse. I'd spank her before I claimed it. I'd have Hilary every which way, and seeing her there, fidgeting and squirming, waiting for my next order, it all made sense.

This was what I'd been waiting for—*she* was what I'd needed. All those floozies in France had been fine, and they'd looked amazing at the end of my cock, beautiful on my arm even, but I'd never felt anything for them, not a flicker of real emotion. The feelings conjuring inside me now were something else. I actually felt a tug of real need when I gazed at her, and it wasn't just lust. I might be a superficial bastard, but I wasn't entirely one dimensional. I knew about emotions—how to identify them, play them, and exploit them—and the ones stirring in me made me giddy. There was something about Hilary. Yes, I wanted to tan that sweet behind and screw her senseless, but after, there was something that made me want to wrap my arms around her, pull her heat to me, and share a moment of intimacy. I shook my head at that startling realization—*I* wanted to be intimate with her.

Me, Sean Hyland.

What would the guys in Nice think of me now?

"You look sensational, by the way." She twisted at the compliment, her eyes wide, though I couldn't decide if it was fervor or fear I saw flickering there. "I like the way your tits jut out." I grinned. "It's very becoming." A fresh blush rose to her cheeks, and this time it was definitely indignation I saw dancing in her irises. "I think we need to consider keeping you this way more often, especially when we're married."

Her brows knitted at the marital reference, and her right foot stomped into the wooden floor, but I smiled at the display of defiance. I liked Hilary's strength, I always had, and though I would tame the fire roaring inside her, I would never extinguish it completely.

"Settle down," I growled, though there was no real intent in my tone. "Settle down, and we'll talk."

Hilary

"I'm sorry about the décor." He proffered the apology as he slid the lock against the door behind him and came to join me in the center of the room. "It was Zander's choice. Very..." He hesitated, his nose crinkling as he tried to think of the right words. "Seventies."

I might have laughed had my mouth not been gagged, and I wasn't reeling from the skin-crawling ignominy of being seen this way in front of those other guys. It was bad enough Sean had seen me this way and that unscrupulous doctor of his. I could scarcely even wrap my head around the way I looked, but now, another two strangers had completed my debasement. My shoulders fell at the thought.

As though he could sense where my muse was going, he reached behind me and tugged loose the buckle at the back of my head. The straps that had held the gag in place fell free at either side of my mouth, leaving only my teeth clinging to the ball.

"Drop it." He held out his palm under my mouth, and acting every inch the obedient puppy he craved, I let the thing fall onto his waiting flesh. His fingers closed around the ball, and he threw it onto the huge desk behind him. "Better?"

There was the sardonic tone again, the one that made me want to fucking kill him.

"Yes, Sir. Thank you."

He nodded, reaching into his jacket and producing a tiny silver key.

"Time to set you free." He sounded almost disappointed as he rounded my body and lifted my wrists higher behind my back. "Let me remind you, one false move, and I will have you chained to me permanently."

I heard the lock turn, and a moment later, he eased first one, then both of my wrists from the cuffs. I brought them up to my face, assessing my flesh for evidence of the bondage.

"I mean it." Sean completed the circle and was back in front of me in a heartbeat. "I won't hesitate to keep you that way, Hilary. In fact, I'd rather enjoy it."

I swallowed at the surety in his voice and believed him. No doubt, he did want a woman chained to his side—one he could flaunt and humiliate on demand, one to keep his cock hard and well-polished—but I wasn't that woman. Even if I had been insanely turned on by some of the outrageous things he'd done to me, that didn't mean I was his. It didn't mean I wanted to be his.

"I understand, Sir."

That knowledge didn't help me. I was still here, locked in Zander Hyland's old office, at the beck and call of his nephew. I had to play the long game if I was going to get out of this. I had to be smart.

"Good." He slipped the cuffs and key back into his jacket pocket. "Would you like a drink?"

My brow rose at the query. It was about the first normal thing he'd said to me since the coffee house.

"Yes, please, Sir." I never got that glass of water earlier, and frankly, the dehydration was starting to show. My head ached, and I was absolutely exhausted.

Lifting his index finger, he pointed it in my direction. "Stay."

I wanted to balk at the derisory order, but I pressed my lips together, watching him as he moved to a nearby dresser.

"Zander had the most rudimentary taste in alcohol, I'm afraid. There's neither a bottle of fizz nor a decent wine selection, but I can offer you a bourbon." He glanced back to me with a half-smile. "I brought this bottle myself."

"Thank you, Sir." I shifted my weight from one foot to the next. "Can I have a glass of water as well?"

He poured the liquor into two glass tumblers, presumably taking his time while I was compelled to await his verdict. Once he'd placed the bottle back on the counter, he lifted one tumbler to his nose and inhaled.

"Ah, that's just what I need."

Lowering my gaze, I didn't reply. I was unsure what he wanted me to say.

"Come over here on your hands and knees, and you may have some." One dark eyebrow rose at the command, and he beckoned me forward with his free hand. "Once you please me, you may have your water."

So, this was the new game then? The public disgracing might be over, but now it was time for Hilary to jump through new hoops for Sean's pleasure. A complicated myriad of emotions knotted inside me as the instruction registered. In isolation, I coped with any part of what he'd suggested. I could kneel and crawl for him. Hell, I'd enjoyed doing some of those things with Saul, but it was the fact Sean was the one asking—he'd taken me without my permission, and there was an underlying assumption I'd just roll over and do every fucking thing he demanded, including marrying him—that was what riled me, and that was what was on my mind as I fell to my knees.

"That's it." His handsome features shifted into a smirk. "Good girl."

I ignored the debilitating fury that wanted to rise at his condescending tone, dismissing it along with the way my clitoris throbbed at his praise. This was just fucked-up and ridiculous. I couldn't get angry and lose my shit with him, but equally, I refused to believe I was finding anything about this sexy. Being kidnapped was not arousing. Being forced into a life with this monster of a man was nothing but immoral lunacy. Perhaps it was testament to how long I'd spent in Saul's company that I'd survived what had happened so far. Maybe that was the cause of my perverse responses. I couldn't accept it was only me—that I was just the twisted woman who got her rocks off, degrading herself for the likes of Sean Hyland.

Pressing my hands into the worn carpet, I tried not to think about his arrogant expression or what else had transpired in this same spot over the years. In fact, I muted all my responses, thinking only of moving one hand and knee at a time as I moved in his direction. By the time his shoes came into view, the motion had become a little easier, though the embarrassment of being made to crawl this way for his pleasure had not.

"Beautiful." He sounded pleased and lifting my head, his face wasn't half as smug as I'd expected. "Here." He reached for the second tumbler and thrust it at me.

I took it in my hands, my gaze following it as I contemplated the amber liquor inside.

"Thank you, Sir."

"Take a sip, then give it back to me." There was excitement in his tone, and already, I knew he was concocting something even worse for me—something awful.

Unthinkingly I obeyed, pressing the glass to my lips and inhaling. The scent of alcohol was intoxicating, sending messages to my brain—this would either give me the confidence to endure whatever was to come or make me hurl. I tipped a small quantity into my mouth before I had time to consider which would win, then handed it back to his outstretched fingers as the drink burned a path down my parched throat.

"Now for water." Sean turned, opening a wood-paneled door to reveal a small refrigerator. Choosing another glass, he collected the spring water from the chiller and poured some. "You may have some when you have paid homage to your husband to be."

Resting on my haunches, I gazed up at him, uncertain and confused. The liquor had sent my senses reeling, and while the initial reaction to be sick had passed, even the tiny amount I'd swallowed had left me heady.

"I don't know what you mean, Sir." My cheeks burned at the admission, and I wondered if this was all part of the game —how to belittle the blonde further.

"It's easy," he answered, though I refused to meet his gaze this time. "Get down there and kiss my feet. It's been a few days since those shoes were buffed, but I can assure you, they're very expensive. Your mouth can do the job for me while I enjoy my bourbon, then once your mouth is full of leather and polish, you can wash it all down with both drinks."

I froze at his words, hearing them, but somehow, unable to comprehend the things he suggested. He wanted me to polish his shoes with my tongue—was that what he was saying?

"You may as well get used to it," he told me with a dry laugh. "You're going to be my wife, and that role will require regular devotion of this sort. When you get good, I might even ask you to do it in front of the guys. That way, you all get a reminder of who's in charge."

Anxiety twisted in my belly, merging with that hot, twisted need that rose from my core and seemed impossible to ignore. He wanted me to degrade myself, which was terrible enough, but for some crazy reason, I responded not only with shock and disgust but with slick, irrefutable need. I wanted to do the things he commanded. I wanted to humble myself for him, and once it was done, and he was happy, I wanted him to put me out of my misery and fuck this burning desire out of me.

I might never be able to look myself in the face again, but there was no point denying what was patently true. Lying to myself wouldn't get me out of this place. It wouldn't get me away from Sean, Saul, and all the other fucked-up immoral men I'd met over the years. Only my compliance would buy that chance. If I did as I was told and earned his trust, maybe, just maybe, my opportunity would come.

CHAPTER 15: SEAN

My balls ached at the sight of her on her hands and knees, gazing up at me through those damp lashes, breasts exposed, and fucking tantalizing. Hilary was a walking wet dream.

"If I have to ask you again, there will be consequences." I glanced away, running my gaze over the terrible furniture. I really had to redecorate this place as soon as I could. I loved my uncle, but jeez, his taste was awful.

"I can't do this." She coughed the words between my shoes. "Please, don't make me, Sir."

"Of course, you can do it," I coaxed, wishing I could adjust my shaft again. Being this hard all the time was proving to be difficult. Not only was it clouding my judgment, but it made basic things like sitting comfortably impossible. "You might not want to do it, but that's not the same thing. You're going to have to do a lot of things you don't want to do to live with me." She trembled at the threat, pulling in a deep breath before her face lowered toward my shoe leather.

"I don't want to do this." Her voice was choked with emotion.

"I know." By contrast, my tone was clipped. "But you're still going to, darling, and that's the point. I am your world now, Hilary. It's time to pay the piper."

Hilary blew out a breath before she pressed her mouth against the expensive Italian leather. Fleetingly, my mind flitted to the Milan store where I'd bought the pair and the pretty little brunette who'd served me, but the groaning blonde at my feet soon drew my attention back to the present.

"Oh, God." She sniffed. "Oh God, I can't believe this."

"Shhh." I took a sip of my drink, reaching down to run my fingers through her blonde locks. Her hair was so soft, just like her skin, and my balls tightened in response. I wanted her, I wanted her so badly, but I wouldn't go down that road yet. I wouldn't take Hilary by force. She wouldn't have my cock until she was desperate and begging for it, and ideally, once I had a ring on her finger. "You're doing great, gorgeous girl. Just keep going."

Her body stilled at my praise, her gaze rising to meet mine.

"It's okay." I smiled as I reassured her. "You're going to polish my shoes for me like a good girl, and while you do, I'll call the appropriate officials and get the wedding plans underway."

"It's really going to happen, then?" She sounded shell-shocked. "You still want to marry me?"

"Of course, beautiful." I held her focus for a moment before my index finger pointed at the floor. "Now, get to it. Kiss the shoes of your master."

Hilary swallowed as though the command was resonating through her.

"Yes, Sir."

It took a few seconds for her to move again, but when she

did, the motion was lither than before, swift, smooth, and if I didn't know better, practiced. She lowered her mouth back to the leather and pressed her lips into it, kissing it over and over again. It was utter fucking perfection.

Reaching into my pocket, I pulled out my phone and dialed Cole's number.

"Mr. Hyland?" His experienced tone echoed back at me. "How can I help you?"

"I need someone to make some arrangements for me." I hesitated for a second, ordering my thoughts away from the sexy-as-fuck look of Hilary at my feet. "I know it's not your remit, but I don't have the right people in place yet."

"It's no problem, Sir." I could hear the smile in his voice, the desire to please me, and at that moment, I was resolved. I'd promote Cole. He was far too good to only be a driver. A loyal man like him deserved more than just the interior of one of Zander's cars. "I'd be happy to help. What arrangements can I make for you?"

"A wedding." Hilary's mouth paused at my shoe, her body tense. "I need someone to marry me and push through all the appropriate paperwork as soon as possible."

"A wedding, Sir?" I could hear the surprise in his tone, but he did his best to hide it.

"That's right. As soon as possible."

"Very good, Sir." In the end, it was Cole's age-old professionalism that won out. "Leave it with me, and I'll have details for you soon."

"Perfect." My smile widened at his cool composure. I needed more men like this. "Keep in touch."

Hanging up the phone, I slipped the device back into my pocket. I'd call my lawyer and get the pre-nuptial papers drawn up soon, but now, there was a hot little woman demanding my attention. My concentration fell to Hilary, and I watched, mesmerized by her performance—the way she dragged her pretty little mouth over the shoes, her breath ragged, and if I didn't know better, the way she wriggled her arse provocatively as she shimmied to pay homage to the other shoe. Was it possible she was enjoying this submission? Reveling in the act of denigrating herself for me?

Could I be that fucking lucky?

"Very nice," I cooed. "Are they cleaner now?"

She drew away, panting as she regarded the leather. "A little, Sir."

"Up on your knees," I instructed, arousal ratcheting up as her breasts swung at my command. "Let me look."

I forced my gaze down past her intoxicating body to the leather. It was slightly cleaner than before, the evidence of the places she'd kissed still visible in places. Not bad for a first attempt. "Good try, little girl."

"Thank you, Sir."

What was that purr in her voice? Was my precious little blonde bride-to-be flirting with me?

"I think you're going to get very good at polishing these shoes for me." I met her coy gaze once more. "Once we're somewhere more private, you can show me some real devotion by kissing my feet as well."

She pulled in a deep breath, shifting on her knees.

"I don't know why, but the idea of those things makes me really horny. Sir." Her focus fell with the confession, the blush at her face burning brighter.

"Is that right?" Placing my drink on the counter behind me, I leaned forward, reaching out to grasp her delicious nipples with both hands. I was Sean Hyland, used to getting what I wanted, but even by my own twisted standards, this was something else. This show of surrender and the way it made me feel was extraordinary, and the thought that Hilary was actually enjoying being humbled was too much—too flawless to be true. "How horny?"

She pulled her lower lip between her teeth. "Very."

"That's most pleasing to hear." I leaned down, gently pressing my forehead to her temple. "I want to do really bad things with you, Hilary, but I won't do any of them without your consent."

"You mean it?"

She blinked at me, breathless and needy in that hedonistic concoction that made me want to pull her onto my cock and break the only rule I'd cemented in my head—I wouldn't take her until the time was right, and in my heart, I knew that time would be once we were married.

"Yes." My tone was emphatic. "I won't force you into sex without consent."

"But you'll force me into marriage?" She arched a brow in that way I often employed. It was the first time anyone had used the gesture at me, and for a second, I was stunned. "You're okay with that, though?"

How dare she look at me that way? How dare she use that tone of voice with me?

"It doesn't seem like you've learned a great deal at my feet, young lady."

She shriveled under the scrutiny of my gaze.

"I… I didn't mean it like that, Sir. I'm sorry." Her expression fell. "I only meant it doesn't seem right to compel someone into wedlock. Marriage is a big commitment."

"Yes." I drew away, nodding at her sentiment. "It's a lifelong one." I pinched her nipples, my balls tightening at the tiny gasp that escaped her lips.

"And you still want to do it?" She lurched forward as I tugged on the sensitive tissue, pulling her closer to the place I was standing. "You still want to make that commitment to me—someone you hadn't even met until the coffee shop?"

My lips twitched at her analysis. She was right, of course. On the surface, nothing about my plan made any sense, but it was what I wanted—Hilary, bound, naked, and subservient, the perfect, hot little wife I could control. Naturally, I'd still take other women whenever I wanted them. Fidelity was not for me, but that didn't mean I didn't want a pretty little thing to come home to. Or maybe I'd bring her to work every day and keep her chained at my desk for when my shoes needed polishing… or my cock.

"I do." I smirked at the irony of my answer, releasing her nipples, and despite her predicament, she even managed a smile.

"Do you know how crazy that sounds?" Her gaze found mine, lingering for a moment. "Sir."

I chuckled at her reasoning. It did sound insane, but there it was, my whole sordid plan laid out for all the universe to see. She would be my submissive, sexy wife, and I would be her rock, her husband—her world.

CHAPTER 16: HILARY

Time protracted, the hours bleeding into days, though I had no conception of what they meant or how they were measured. I didn't know where I was or how long I'd been here. I didn't know if Saul was out there, looking for me, or whether I'd been forgotten, like so many women before me. I'd seen them come and go, the flimsy females who hung off the arms of the men I'd worked with at The Syndicate. They were disposable, just like the lifestyle, but I'd thought things had been different with Saul and me. Before this, before I'd been taken, I'd thought…

What did it matter anymore? Nothing made sense, except Sean, except the fire in his eyes and the way my blood heated at his touch, that and the constant battle playing out in my head. The woman I'd been before—with Saul—the one who liked to dress up, make the best of herself, work and play hard, warring with the submissive mess I seemed to have become.

I didn't want to marry Sean. Of course, I didn't. For fuck's sake, I didn't want to get married at all, but I couldn't deny the electricity between us… perhaps that wasn't true. Maybe it could be refuted, and I just didn't want to. Trapped in the confines he set for me, I didn't know anymore.

"Lost in thought?" I turned at the sound of his voice, my eyes adjusting as they searched the dark contours of the room.

Somewhere in the back of my mind, I thought this was a penthouse, some expensive place he was renting—I thought that was what he'd told me—but I couldn't be sure. I hadn't had a decent sleep since he took me, and the place was always in shadows as if he was intentionally robbing me of daylight and the sense of time it afforded.

"I'm tired." I wanted to lift my hand and rub my temples, but that wasn't an option. "Sir."

He still insisted I use the overinflated title for him, and somehow, I was heady each time I did—even though it was bullshit. Hilary Mantle didn't take orders from any man. She was no one's slave, yet my reality begged to differ. I had been torn from the life I'd known, forced into virtual nudity, save for the collar he insisted I wear around my neck like some sort of animal and the cuffs he often demanded at my wrists and ankles. Nothing about me was vaguely reminiscent of the woman I had been, and still, he talked about marriage as though it was the obvious choice for a woman kidnapped and chained in this dark place.

"Things will be different soon." His voice floated past me, surreal to a point, I wondered if I'd been drugged again. Maybe he was slipping something into the water he offered, something to calm and placate me. Something that kept the defiance at bay every time he humiliated me further. "Better."

"Better how?" In some ways, I didn't know why I asked. Things had to get better than this, didn't they? There had to be a life beyond these four black walls. If I truly didn't believe that I'd have gone insane by now, wouldn't I?

Sanity.

That was an interesting question, all things considered.

Perhaps I had lost my mind already, and that was why I was so placid? Maybe he wasn't sedating me at all. Insanity was always portrayed as violent lunacy, but who was to say it had to be? I always had to do things differently. I wore bright pinks when goths were in fashion, and I refused to listen to the tripe they called modern music. I was my own woman… at least, I used to be. If I was losing my marbles, it would stand to reason this was how I'd behave.

"Better when we're man and wife."

Not this again. My hands balled into fists, my fingernails cutting into my skin. Why was he always banging the marriage drum? Marriage was not going to save us. For God's sake, years of intensive therapy might not even be enough.

"Will I have to stay here then, Sir?" I'd already learned there was little point in countering him. My fiery outbursts only led to more punishments concocted by his dark and devious mind. There seemed no limit to what he could conjure, no end to the depravity he would pour over me. "Once we're married."

Sean moved into my line of sight, his blue eyes alight with emotion, though it was impossible to say which. His moods seemed to swing between anger, resentment, and unbridled lust.

"No." He pressed his hands down either side of the chair I was chained to, the sinews in his forearms visible from the shadows. "No, once you're legally mine, things will change. We'll get a place together."

I gazed up at his pensive stare. A place together? Was he fucking serious? It didn't matter how good the sex was—I wasn't staying around to be his little wife! No man in the world was worth all this shit. I had a life out there somewhere. Friends I missed, a job I liked, and a boss I'd been happy fucking, then one day, Sean Hyland came along and made it all disappear. *Poof*—just like that.

"Oh." In the end, there was nothing else to say, nothing that would make a difference—nothing that would take away the pain of the stark reality. Sean had held me for God knew how long, treated me in the basest ways, and for some fucked-up reason, I'd responded. Hell, I'd even been stupid enough to tell him how being on my hands and knees made me feel—what on earth was wrong with me?

"When, Sir? When will we marry?"

His grin widened, revealing that pearl-white line of teeth, like someone on a dental hygiene advert.

"I'm glad you asked." He tilted his head at me. "It's nice to see you a little keener about the idea."

I blinked at him, uncertain how to respond. I knew what I wanted to say. I wanted to laugh at his arrogant response—at the assumption, I suddenly chose him, that I sought this ridiculous union. What I craved was his electrifying caress, the knot of energy that twisted whenever he commanded me to debase myself for him again. I hated to admit it, but the approval in his tone and the satisfaction in his eyes were my drivers. I had no desire to become his wife, or anyone else's, but if it was what I had to do to get the hell out of this debilitating limbo, I had reconciled myself to the idea. I would be his wife. To get out of this hellhole, to get away from his clutches, I would do whatever I had to do.

"I've been giving it a lot of thought," I whispered into his chin. "Maybe it will be for the best."

"Oh, it will be." He grinned at the answer he wanted to hear. "You will make such a beautiful bride. Just wait until you see the dress I have chosen for you."

Anxiety churned in my belly at what that might mean, but there was little time to dwell on it. He was already undoing the leather at my left wrist, releasing me from the chair I'd been strapped to in the gloom. My breathing accelerated as he liberated my second wrist, relief at my freedom mingling with apprehension about what was to come. Sean only ever set me free for one reason, and that was erotic torment. At first, I'd been worried he'd go back on his word and take what he wanted from me by force, but time had proven those fears to be ill-founded.

Sean, it seemed, had no intention of violating me. His endeavor was all about my anguish. He degraded me, knowing I would revel in the acts he compelled, yet since that first night in the basement at Hyland's headquarters, he'd never let me come again. He whipped up my desire to within an inch of lucidity and left me hanging, taking me to the edge over and over and never satisfying. It was captivating in all the wrong ways.

"Down on your knees." He rose to his full height, gesturing toward the floor, and like the well-trained animal I'd become, I complied, lifting myself from the seat, which had become my captor for so long, and sinking to my knees. "Good. It's time to continue your training."

I glanced down at his shoes, every muscle in my body tensing at his warning. We'd started this so-called training a while ago, and now kissing his feet seemed like the best of an undeniably hot yet unbelievably awful selection. I'd lowered myself to feed his desires, and the worst of it was I fucking loved it. My clit throbbed at the haunting memories, just as it pulsed at the nefarious glint in his eyes.

"Now…" His voice boomed around me, like the thunderous roar of God. "Where did we get to?"

I exhaled, loathing this part the most. Acting out the

insane and debauched things he asked was one thing, but having to talk about them—vocalize them—was debilitating.

"Y-You were teaching me how to be a good wife." My face flamed, hating how pathetic I sounded, yet already aware of the pang of longing between my legs. "Preparing me."

"Oh, yes." Sean chuckled. "So, we have covered daily devotion. You know I expect you to kiss and lick my feet."

I gulped at the way he made that sound, recalling how much I despised and adored the act he referred to. I hated feet, always would, but humbling myself for his enjoyment was something I relished.

"Yes, Sir."

"What next, I wonder?" He lowered to his haunches, capturing my chin between his thumb and index finger. "How else should a wife serve her husband?"

There it was—the query he always asked, already knowing how I was instructed to respond. "However you tell her, Sir."

"Very good." He stroked my chin idly. "You *have* been paying attention." Rising to his feet, he strode to a table at the far wall. In the darkness, it was impossible to see what was on there, but the thing was always laden with implements designed to make me suffer. I held my breath, knowing whatever he chose would signal my imminent fate.

"Here we are." He held a black item aloft, and it took a second for my eyes to determine what it was, my stomach clenching when the gag finally came into view. It was black, just like the ball gag he'd shoved in my mouth all those times, but this one was different. The front was flat aside from a few black ridges, but as he spun it around, I could see the other side was a black dildo, about three inches in length, smooth, black plastic.

"A good wife is silent." He winked at me. "She knows her place, and where is that, Hilary?"

"At her husband's feet, Sir." I didn't believe a word, but boy, did it turn me on to feign it. This was what he wanted, but I got off on it as well.

"That's right." He smiled, waving the gag in front of my eyes, but his approving tone was enough to quell the unease, to make it all worthwhile. "Quiet, subservient, and on her knees."

CHAPTER 17: SEAN

She was fucking flawless. I had sensed it right from that first coffee stain, but kneeling there, labored breaths, great tits, and wide eyes, Hilary proved it all over again. I had spent the best part of the last four days bringing her to heel. Taking only essential meetings and delegating most other tasks, I probably wasn't doing the Hyland name justice, but at the moment, my focus was blinkered. It didn't matter what I was doing, who I was talking to, or what shit I was trying to sort. In my mind's eye, all I could see was the reverence in her gaze when I had her right on the edge, all I could taste was the flavor of her skin, the palate of her perfect pussy juices on my tongue, and all I could hear were her muffled cries and the scintillating way she begged for release I would never allow.

Keeping Hilary so close to hedonism was proving a potent technique. I kept her bound for the most part, to a degree, because I simply adored the bondage but also because it was the only way I could guarantee she wasn't playing with her pretty cunt, satiating those flames in my absence. I licked my lips at just how tightly wound my bride-to-be was. I'd noticed over the last couple of days, she'd become all the more willing to play my devilish games, desperate as she was for release. For some foolish reason, she seemed to be under the impression I might take pity on her, when in truth, all I planned to do was play and tease her, ensuring I emptied my cum all over her eager tongue, tits, or arse.

"There will be plenty of times in our married life when I have work responsibilities." I ruffled her hair playfully. "I'm sure you understand." She ought to, based on her previous work experience.

Her gaze rose momentarily. "Yes, Sir."

"At those times, you will be expected to serve me but will need to remain silent and passive."

She inhaled with a slight nod. Being quiet and submissive were traits Hilary had practiced a lot lately.

"For example, I might have an important business meeting, but obviously, as a devoted husband, I would not want to leave you, so…" I arched my eyebrow at her. "I might gag you and have you perform the role of my personal footrest for the duration of the conference."

Her lips parted at my suggestion, her face blanching.

"A footrest, Sir?" Her voice quivered, demonstrating her evident trepidation.

"To begin with," I agreed. "We would graduate to a table, but not straight off the bat. We wouldn't want you spilling all those drinks, would we?" Wide, blue eyes stared in my direction as though she couldn't believe what she was hearing.

"I asked you a question, Hilary," I prompted.

"No, Sir," she answered at once. "But how could I possibly be a table? I wouldn't be able to move at all?"

"Pretty much," I concurred with a grin. "The secret is a nice flat, tabletop. That's what you need to master, what the footrest exercise is good for, and that's why we begin the learning today. I wouldn't want you showing me up in front of all my associates." I winked at her, relishing the burning hue that colored her face as if I'd commanded it. Even in the shadows, her embarrassment resonated. Hilary blushed with such blissful ease. It was wonderful. "You will drink before we begin."

Turning from her, I wandered the short distance to the small refrigerator in the corner and took out her bowl and a bottle of water. I flicked on a small corner spotlight, enough illumination to enjoy the look of Hilary, but not enough to indulge her. This was a temporary place for us, a stylish enough penthouse I could rent while we waited for the wedding and before we found somewhere more permanent. I'd had this room decorated with sensory deprivation in mind and had moved her in straight away. Constantly warm, it was decked out with security cameras at every angle, so I could keep a close eye on her, even when I had to leave, but more than that, it was safe. Most of my own men didn't know she was here, let alone anyone else, which meant I didn't have to worry about Morrison turning up for an unexpected rescue attempt.

"Here you go." I paced back to the place she knelt, her knees parted, just the way I'd taught her, revealing a gleaming pussy, and bit back the smile that rose at the sight. Even now, under all the erotic duress I could muster, she was fabulously turned on, and I knew if I swept a finger over her pussy, I'd find out for myself. Placing the metallic bowl on the ground in front of her, I opened the bottle and emptied half of the contents into it before taking a step back and draining the remainder. I'd never been an avid fan of pet play, but I did so enjoy degrading her, and the expression on her face made the whole thing worthwhile.

"Drink up."

She sighed. "But I'm no good at this, Sir. Remember what a mess I made before?"

"Yes, I do recall." I sniggered at the recollection. "That's why you earned yourself a good, hard spanking and also why I have decent hard flooring in here."

Hilary met my gaze, her countenance forlorn.

"But you still want me to do it again, Sir?"

Why was she even asking? Wasn't it abundantly clear what I expected?

"Of course," I replied with glee. "We do not improve unless we practice, do we?"

"No, Sir." Her expression crumbled further as the realization of what awaited came crashing down.

"Come on, then," I goaded. "Get to it. Lap with your tongue like a good little animal, and maybe I won't make you finish the whole bowl before I gag you."

A glimmer of emotion sparkled in her gaze, but the old pride and defiance weren't among them. It seemed a few days in my care had done almost enough to stifle them completely. Now Hilary was almost as desperate to please as she was to come. She lowered her head to the bowl and lapped admirably at the contents, but inevitably, little of the liquid made it past her lips. Naturally, it wasn't her fault, human tongues were hardly designed for the purpose, but it was enormously delectable to witness, my cock straining to be free of the attire that confined it. I crouched beside her, pulling back the length of her tresses which gravity had taken into the water.

"Very pretty, Hilary. You make a delightful pet."

Her face flamed at the compliment, but she didn't stop, her tongue continuing its humiliating hunt into the bowl as she tried, largely futilely, to consume as much as she could.

"Enough." The one word brought events to a halt. "Crawl to my comfy chair. It's time you were useful once more."

Her focus flitted to the corner, which housed the large comfortable chair, and the only portion of the room that was carpeted, and slowly, she began to move, sliding one hand in front of one knee as her tortuous crawl went on. I strode ahead of her, clutching the gag, and ensured I was seated by the time she arrived.

"No lesson in silence is complete without a gag." I lifted the black plastic into the air above her head. "Present your mouth for the purpose."

There was reticence at first, an obvious reluctance to open her mouth and submit to the gag, and I could understand why. Hilary had just about come to terms with the ball gag, but this thing was something else. The dildo part would ensure there was no chance of mumbling around the plastic. Its plastic shaft would fit snugly down her throat for the entirety of the lesson.

"If you keep me waiting, I might consider leaving the gag in place when I leave..." My brow rose with threat, and quick as a flash, her lips parted enough for me to slide the end of the plastic past them. "Better," I snapped. "Now, relax, and let it in. Fighting will only make things worse."

Panic pinballed in her eyes as I pulled the straps into place on either side of her head, and by the time I fastened it in place, her breathing was ragged.

"Calm," I reminded her, leaning back to take in the view. Her lips were stretched wide around the rim of the gag, the front part fitted with special features, which meant other adaptions could be locked into place. My arousal soared as I imagined the cup holder or various other functions she could serve while being gagged this way. "Making yourself choke around the thing won't do you any favors. As you can tell, it's not long enough to do you any harm, only to keep that mouth full and silent." I waited a moment for her to settle and a sweet look of resignation to fall over her face.

"Good," I praised. "Now, onto all fours in front of me." I spread my legs wide, offering her the space she needed to crawl into place, and with one terrified glance in my direction, she complied. "All you need to do now is stay exactly where you are." I grinned, lifting one, then the other leg into place on her back. I was careful to ensure I moved gently, and it was my calves rather than my heels that grazed her delicate flesh. I was exactly where I needed to be—sitting comfortably after a long day of work, using my gagged and naked woman as a footrest. Smiling, I tilted my head back in the high-backed chair.

Everything was going to plan. The wedding was booked for next Thursday, a small affair where Zander's personal friend, Olly, a qualified registrar, would perform the legal ceremony. My lawyer had been in touch to confirm the appropriate paperwork would all be ready by then, and of course, the gracious Miss Mantle would be signing away her rights to my money at the same time she signed the marriage certificate. That's all she'd be doing with her hands, though. They'd be shackled most of the day in the beautiful ivory chains I'd ordered. They matched the rest of her skimpy outfit perfectly, where every inch of the woman I now owned would be on display, and naturally, I purchased a wonderful white ballgag, collar, and veil for the purpose.

Hilary would be quite the picture on her special day.

I couldn't fucking wait.

"This is how it will be every night," I explained, smiling at the mental image of my bride crawling down the aisle to my side. "Perhaps I will have you kiss my feet first, or maybe that comes afterward, but once we're home, you will serve me a meal, then busy yourself with your other roles, furniture being one."

She pulled air through her nose, and I noticed how her muscles tensed, but any attempt at resistance for Hilary was over. I was in charge of her destiny now. Reaching for my phone, I switched on the camera and took a number of new shots of her below my feet for my collection. One day, Saul would receive a barrage of photos of his ex-girlfriend. I'd resisted the urge to send any yet, preferring to marry her first, so for now, they remained for my private consumption only.

Just like Hilary.

CHAPTER 18: SAUL MORRISON

Five days. It had been five fucking days since I'd seen her. Five days. Five long days of angst and concern. The kind of anxiety that physically hurt, that left me unable to eat, sleep, or function. That had been my life, my everything since Hilary vanished. I'd never realized what she meant, never taken the time to breathe in the scent of her honeyed tresses or gaze into her eyes and tell her how much I needed her. The sex had started casually, though I'd desired her for years, and within a day or two, it became consuming. She took over my body and mind, my only waking thought and every carnal need. In the short time we spent together, I had fallen head over heels. For the first time in so many years, Saul Morrison was in love.

Then she was gone, disappearing completely as if she'd been wiped off the face of the planet, but I knew she hadn't. People didn't just vanish, even in our world—something had happened to her. *Someone* happened, and my churning trepidation had an idea it was linked to Zander Hyland. That man had been the bane of my existence when he was alive, and even taking the motherfucker out wasn't enough to save me from his poison. I couldn't prove it yet, but somehow, I knew. This had Hyland's grubby fingerprints all over it, and as soon as I could connect the dots, I would wipe out whoever was left in the nest he'd created.

That didn't help me, though, and it sure as hell didn't help Hilary. I knew the type of cretins who worked for Hyland. They were the worst kind of men, the sort who'd do anything. Furious fear knotted in my stomach at the thought of what might be happening to her. That was why I couldn't rest until she was safe. Whether she reciprocated my feelings or not, I owed Hilary that much.

The buzz of my phone derailed my spiraling thoughts, and glancing down at the screen, I saw the name I'd been waiting for flashing in front of me.

"Craig?" I answered eagerly, wanting desperately for the man I'd planted inside Hyland's organization to have some good news, but sensing that was a vain hope. "Do you have an update?"

"Yes." He sounded tired, but weren't we all? "It's taken a couple of days to find someone I can trust. Most of my contacts were taken out in the stand-off between you and Zander, and I—"

"Okay, Craig, cut to the chase." My jaw clenched at the way I berated him, a twinge of guilt twisting in my chest. I liked Lauper, and he'd been loyal to me, providing a wealth of useful information on my rivals over the years, but I couldn't help it. My affection for Hilary was too great. Whatever he knew, I coveted that power.

I wanted her back.

"I'm sorry. I don't mean to snap, but please… tell me what you know." The tension was rising in my chest, threatening to compress my heart and cut off my oxygen supply altogether.

"It's okay." I could hear the compassion in his voice. "I know you care about Hilary, and she's okay."

"Really? Where is she? Is she safe?" The questions rolled off my tongue faster than my brain could rationalize them, but they were the relevant ones, the ones that haunted me, keeping me awake night after night.

"She's alive, yes," Lauper answered. "Hyland has her."

"Hyland?" The anxiety knotting inside me ratcheted up another notch. "B-But, he's dead. I shot him. I…"

"Not *that*, Hyland, Saul." Lauper's words stopped me in my tracks. "This is his nephew, Sean."

Fuck. For a second, my heart stopped altogether. Sean fucking Hyland, seriously? That little shit had left the country years ago. The last I'd heard, he'd been living it up in France.

"Sean Hyland's back?" Though, even as I asked, it all made sense. Of course, he was back. Sean was back to reclaim the so-called Hyland empire, and somehow, he got to Hilary. "He has her?"

"Yes." Lauper's tone was emphatic. "I still have a couple of guys I trust, and they've told me where he's hiding her."

"Fuck." That time the word escaped my lips. "If he's hurt one fucking hair on her head, I swear, I'm going to rip that little shit into pieces."

"I know."

"How is she?" I gritted my teeth, but the goading thought remained. *How was Hilary? Was she safe? What had that little bastard done to her?* Men like him—like me—didn't take people for fun. He'd snatched her for a reason, and I shuddered at the thought of what that reason might be.

"She's alive, that's all I know. Except…"

My body tensed. "Except what?" I barked. "What, Craig? Tell me what you fucking know."

"There's word he's planning to marry her."

"What?" I panted as the explanation tried to register in my brain.

"He's going to wed her next week, I hear."

"Marry her?" My fingers of my free hand balled into a fist. "What the hell?"

"I know." His tone was resigned. "It's fucked up."

"I have to stop this, have to get to her." The thoughts were coming at me fast, but my brain couldn't rationalize them. Why on earth would Sean Hyland want to marry Hilary? Of course, she was beautiful, smart, and sexy. She was kind, too. She cared about people in a way that was rare in this business. I knew he'd want to fuck her, and that concept made me want to spit blood. I swore to all that was holy, I would make him pay for any harm he'd caused her, but more than that, the idea of marriage was an insult, to Hilary, to the institution, to me…

It hit me then.

That was what this was about.

It was about me, about *insulting me.*

I'd killed his uncle, and in spite, he took my woman, but it wasn't enough to hold her, to have her…

My head fell, my knees buckling as recognition permeated my senses. Hyland wanted to do more than just take what was mine. He wanted to own it, and in his twisted mind, marrying Hilary was how he'd achieve it.

"He's doing it to get back at me. It's about insulting me."

"You're right." There was silence for a moment. "I'm sure you're right. What do you want to do?"

I inhaled, trying to get enough oxygen to my brain, but my every judgment was clouded. I could scarcely think.

"I don't know." It pained me to admit it. "I don't know, but something… I'll think of something. I have to get her back. She shouldn't suffer because of me."

"Okay. Think about it. Call me when you know. I'll keep my ear to the ground at this end."

"Thanks, Craig." I needed men like Lauper more than ever. "I'll be in touch."

Ending the call, I slumped back into my chair and threw the device onto my desk, spinning in my chair to take in the London skyline. My office boasted an impressive panorama of the cityscape, and at this time of day, when the sun set, there were few more inspiring views, but the scene held little motivation for me now.

Without Hilary, I was bereft. I could round up my troops, get Dalton, Connor, and Manuel to help get her back, but I couldn't deny what was flagrantly clear. Sean Hyland was back in the country for one purpose only. He wanted another war, a war I thought I'd just put to bed with a bullet to Zander's brain. A war I'd hoped was over forever.

"Hilary," I whispered her name into my chest. "I'm sorry, sweetheart. Don't give up. I'm coming for you. I'm coming."

The End.

Devour Hyland's Consort *for* the next sizzling installment of Hilary and Sean's twisted love affair!

Read the introduction to the book now…

Hyland's Consort
(*A Rage and Revenge Novel*):
A Dark Mafia Dark Necessities Romance.

Book Two
By
Felicity Brandon

Copyright © 2021 by Felicity Brandon

Prologue: Sean Hyland

"You're sure this is what you want?" His expression serious, Crane's fingers paused over the keyboard as he glanced up.

"Are you asking if I'm mentally competent?" I sniggered, amused the man I paid such a huge sum was questioning me.

"I'm asking if you're sure." His fingers went to work again, *tap, tap, tapping* on the plastic keys as he completed the paperwork. "I'd be remiss if I didn't, sir. It's all so…" He paused, apparently trying to think of the right word.

"Sudden?" My brow arched. He was right. The decision to take a wife was abrupt, to say the least, and contrary to the self-serving man I'd become, but Hilary had turned everything upside down. Since I got my hands on her, all I could think about was leading her down the aisle and finally claiming what was mine.

"Precisely." Crane leaned forward, staring at me over his spectacles. "I've known you a long time, Mr. Hyland." His tone was ominous, reminding me of one of my uncle Zander's droning speeches… until Saul Morrison had put a bullet through Zander's brain. "And I knew your uncle even longer. I just want to ensure your interests are protected."

"That's exactly what you're going to do," I assured him, offering the older man a smile. "You'll ensure all Zander's properties and assets are safeguarded in the event of divorce or my death."

"They're your assets now, sir."

"That's right." I sighed, leaning back in the huge black leather seat. I still hadn't wrapped my head around Zander's death, let alone avenged the bastard who'd brought him down, but I would. I was working on both, and my new bride was the pièce de résistance. "Sometimes, it's difficult to think about it that way."

Crane considered me from behind the vast screen. "That's understandable." His tone was sympathetic. "The loss of Mr. Hyland was tragic. None of us want to believe he's gone."

Yet he was gone—murdered in the same grotty London office I was redecorating, brought to heel by the rival gang who'd been the thorn in his side his whole life.

"Still, you're here now." Crane's lips twitched. "The next

generation of Hyland, and I feel sure there're brighter days to come."

"Indeed, there are." I pressed my fingertips together, contemplating the day in question. The wedding was set in only three days, and the documents Crane was putting together were the final loose end to be tied up. "A great many. I thank you for your concern, Mr. Crane, as well as your long service, but my mind is made up. I'm marrying Miss Mantle."

His brow rose at my emphatic tone, but a professional like Crane knew when to argue and when to get the job done. "Very good, sir." He pressed his lips together, attention flitting back to the screen. "Then we're nearly done here. I'll just need a signature from Miss Mantle."

"An electronic one won't suffice?" I already knew the answer, but I asked anyway. Getting Hilary to Crane's office was going to be an interesting challenge. I'd been keeping her in sensory deprivation, edging her closer and closer to ecstasy each time we played but never permitting her to reach the stars. After so long without the light, without hope and longing for my touch, Hilary had become quite the well-trained, eager pup. I could certainly get her to sign the paperwork, but taking her from the place I held her wasn't my preferred option.

"I'm afraid not," he replied. "I could bring the papers to your address if you desire?"

"No, I'll bring her here." I sighed, but even as the air was expelled, my lips curled, imagining my gorgeous blonde scampering around on all fours in Crane's wood-paneled office. "She could use a trip out."

Crane laughed. "Well, I've never heard my offices referred to that way, sir."

My grin widened at his amusement. "These are strange

times, Mr. Crane. I'm certain Hilary will appreciate the chance to meet you."

"Very good," he replied, his focus flitting between the screen and my face. "Does tomorrow suit you both? Better we get this finalized in advance of the wedding, I think."

"Tomorrow is grand."

I envisioned Hilary's slender limbs moving across Crane's old-fashioned carpet and her utter embarrassment at the public humiliation, but she may as well get used to it. Come the big day, she'd be bared and subjugated as much as I desired, and based on the way I was constantly aroused, that could be most of the day.

"What time, Mr. Crane?"

"I have an early slot." He peered around the screen as if checking I was still there. Poor Derek Crane. I'd be willing to wager his office had never seen anything like my bride-to-be. "Nine in the morning?"

I inhaled at the thought of having to drag Hilary here so early. "I can make that work," I agreed, trying to ignore the swell of passion that surged at the thought of Hilary and focusing on the dry, monotonous, but nonetheless significant reasons that brought me to Crane's office. "It will give you the chance to meet my intended and see what all the fuss is about."

"Yes, sir, though I'm sure she's quite the catch. Why else would you want to get her down the aisle so quickly?" He grinned, revealing a line of crooked teeth, and I started to laugh.

"Why else, indeed?"

HYLAND'S CONSORT - CHAPTER 1

Chapter 1: Hilary Mantle

The slither of illumination at the far end of the room edged across the wall. Cast from the tiny space behind the blackout blind, which leaked light, it was only a trickle, but it was all I had. In the days I'd been here, I noticed its pattern and envied it. I resented its routine, begrudged the fact it could move so freely when I could not, but over time, it had come to represent something greater than just the contrast between our fortunes—it began to indicate time. Based on its position, I could work out what time of day it was beyond the endless gloom of the place where he kept me, its presence a fleeting semblance of normality in this new depravity.

Sighing, I watched its slow path, tension knotting in my shoulders. I was naked and bound to the chair again. I was always bound and naked. Tethered and unable to flee, enveloped in sultry shadows and, as usual, right on the edge of reason before I'd been abandoned. Fleetingly, my mind flitted back to the first day Sean Hyland had captured me, to the onslaught I'd been made to endure at his hands, the rounds and rounds of pleasure he'd ripped from my reluctant body in that dank little basement cell. That might as well have been a thousand years ago for all I could recall of the thunderous orgasms. Now, those climaxes were as out of reach as freedom itself. It was the game Sean loved to play—one that enthralled him while leaving me perpetually on the brink of breakdown. Each time he returned, I'd be permitted to move, but liberty came at a price. I'd have to cede to his demented will and allow him access to my body, permit him to torment me. There was no denying Sean could play the game. He was a champion competitor. We'd only just met, yet he was capable of stimulating me in ways most men could hardly conceive, and while he'd refrained from actually taking what he so clearly believed belonged to him, the threat was always there. *I was his.* His to tease, his to harass, his to garner thrills from, and one day, he would expect much more.

My insides tightened at the thought of that day. Sean had made no bones about it. It would be our wedding day, and apparently, it was looming faster than I imagined, though in the confines of this place, even the slither of light couldn't illuminate how soon for me.

"Soon," I whispered into the darkness, pleased for once, he'd permitted me the possibility.

Sean had a penchant for gags and enjoyed seeing me struggle in one. It was all shades of wrong, watching him harden at my dismay at not being able to communicate, but even worse was the pulverizing reality I enjoyed it, too. What could be worse than finding yourself in such a hopeless situation—hostage to the deranged rival of your boss—than discovering you actually relished his insidious attention? But it was true. I'd been wetter and needier than ever fettered in his bondage. Hornier than I'd been with any boyfriend and even needier than I'd been with Saul. My face screwed up at the unpleasant reality. Saul Morrison, the man who'd signed my paychecks for the last three years, was also the same man I'd bedded by choice before this ordeal—the man I thought I'd been in love with.

Where was Saul?

Glancing up, my gaze fixed on the dribble of light visible across the room. Was he out there somewhere, looking for me? Granted, we never got to the stage of saying we loved each other, and I wasn't sure either of us was ready to declare undying devotion, but we'd been pretty damn close. If I knew anything about my lover, he protected everyone in his organization. He'd come for me—I knew he would—he'd never leave me to rot in the darkness with a ruthless cretin like Sean Hyland. That wasn't Saul's style. However, he wouldn't anticipate how deep the rabbit hole had gone, wouldn't dare guess at the devious games Sean played. Never in Saul's wildest dreams would he imagine the nephew of his old gang rival would not only capture me but plan to marry me.

Once I was Mrs. Hyland, where could I go from there? There could be no coming back, no divorce lawyer who could wash away the stain of having actually been his wife. How could I go back to Saul's organization, The Syndicate, after that? How could I go back to his bed? The short answer was, I couldn't. If Sean insisted on this lunacy, he was forcing my hand into more than just marriage. He was imposing an entirely new life on me, a new job, a new social circle—if he ever allowed me out of this bloody room.

A shot of anger raced through me, my impotency swelling

until it was difficult to take another breath. I still couldn't believe this had happened. I'd been content with my life in a job I enjoyed with a decent group of friends. I'd finally found a man who respected me, a man I could envision a real future with, then this had happened. Now I was lucky if I could leave my damn chair, and when I did, Sean had me crouching over a bowl to relieve myself before I begged and pleaded for more of whatever pleased him.

If you'd have told me only a couple of weeks ago that this would be my fate, I'm certain I would have called you crazy, but not only was I Sean's prisoner, in the haze of shadows and craving for the satisfaction he never offered, I couldn't even contemplate how to escape. My head was a mess, spinning with every sound. Was that the creaking floorboard Sean approaching from behind the door? Was he about to arrive and turn my world on its head again?

Yes, he met my basic needs. He ensured I was fed and as clean as water and a sponge could achieve, but this neverending solitude was starting to drive me insane. Hours when only the noise of my frantic heartbeat kept me company, that and the slow progress of the slither of light— my only friend in this dark desolation. It had gotten to the point where I no longer knew what I wanted, wasn't sure if I longed for Sean's arrival, for human interaction, to be free of the chair at least. Or if I craved the boundless hours of seclusion, the time when I only had my thoughts for company.

Nothing seemed real anymore.

Just as the riddle burgeoned, threatening to implode in my mind once and for all, I heard the telltale sound of Sean's imminent arrival, the noise of his tread reverberating until I swore I could actually feel the resonance.

Sean!

Once more, his approach brought with it an odd mixture

of relief and trepidation. He was my only route out of this room. Whatever did or didn't transpire—whether he compelled me to marry him, whether Saul came to my rescue, or in the short term, if I wanted to eat or ever get out of this bloody seat—I needed him in a very tangible way. Then there was the obvious reality of my predicament. Sean was the same man who'd snatched me from outside my home, pumped me full of sedative, and tormented me. There was nothing sane about being eager to see a man like that.

Just when I didn't think the tension twisting inside could intensify any further, the key slid into the lock beyond the door. I'd heard the action countless times before, but still, each time it happened, my heart rate quickened, my throat drying as I tried to anticipate his next move. What mood would he be in when he opened that door? What would he want from me? Aside from the inevitable answer that he relished seeing me struggle, it was impossible to say, but knowing Sean, he wouldn't keep me waiting long.

"There she is." He threw the door open in triumph, my eyes blinking into the muted light it provided. "My bride-to-be."

A shiver ran the length of my spine at his pronouncement. Frankly, I wasn't certain I ever wanted to get married, let alone to some cocky criminal I didn't really know.

"How have you been, gorgeous, a good girl, I hope?"

"Yes, Mr. Hyland, Sir." I blew out a breath, the words he expected falling from my lips without a second thought.

Christ, what had happened to me? A few days in this anguished state and I'd ceded to his will, conditioned like an obedient pet to do his every bidding. The muscles at the apex of my thighs clenched at the debilitating thought. I loathed how he must perceive me—an easy blonde he could tie up and order around—but every time I tried to muster the energy to focus on who I really was, on the responses he deserved, Sean had an answer. An unceremonious trip over his knee for the type of humiliating spanking that left my head spinning and my arse in discomfort when he bound me to the chair again. A humbling request to demean me, often while he videoed the ordeal for so-called prosperity—he seemed to have a response for everything.

"Good girl." He moved inside the room, closing the distance between us in a few strides. "Let me look at you." One hand rose to my chin, pulling it north to meet his demanding eyes. "I have news, Hilary. News which may interest you."

My belly tightened, anxiety pinballing. Anything that interested Sean was bound to mean more trouble for me, more reasons to worry, to cry, to be chastened.

"Want to hear my news?"

I blinked up at him, knowing there was only one acceptable answer.

"Yes, please, Sir."

He lowered to his haunches, the hand at my chin grazing over my exposed breast en route to my knee. My breathing accelerated, my helplessness to prevent his exploration of my body arousing and vexing in equal measure, his sudden proximity doing nothing to assuage my apprehensions.

"It's time to get you out of here." He smiled, one side of his face eerily lit by the subdued light coming from the open doorway. "Time to clean you up. We're going on a little trip tomorrow."

"To get m-married?" I could barely get the words out, but I had to know. He'd repeatedly implied he wanted our nuptials to be as soon as possible, and despite my friendly slither of light, it was possible I'd misjudged the days, that this was it—my time was up.

"No, not yet." He chuckled, tenderly patting my knee as if I said something amusing. "Though it's good to see you're excited about the upcoming big event."

Excitement? Is that what I'd conveyed with my stammering reaction?

"This time, it's a trip to see my legal man, a few documents for my new bride to sign." He leaned closer, edging between my parted knees. "Before you get to sign the important one on the day itself."

My brow furrowed. I still couldn't believe he expected me to play along with this ludicrous plan to get married, but I knew countering him at this juncture wouldn't help my cause. It wouldn't get me out of this chair, or indeed, out of this blasted room, and from the things he said, there was a brief glimmer of hope that his plan might be a way out of here. In the end, I said the one thing I knew would please him, the only thing guaranteed to win his approval.

"Yes, Sir. Thank you."

Devour now!

https://books2read.com/u/4XQnWN

FOLLOW ME!

Stay in touch with Felicity's new releases by subscribing to her mailing list.
https://felicitybrandonwrites.com/newsletter/
You'll also receive FREE reads just for signing up!

Love Dark Romance?

Discover ALL The Dark Necessities **universe!**
https://books2read.com/u/mdGvJd

-

Devour Tempted for FREE:
https://books2read.com/u/b5kPPA

-

Join Felicity's Facebook group, **and** Discord group, **to engage with her and other awesome readers.**